SHATTERED

For my husband, David Baron:
That leap of faith—it was everything.

SHATTERED

Kathi Baron

WestSide Books
Lodi, New Jersey

Published by WestSide Books
60 Industrial Road
Lodi, NJ 07644
973-458-0485
Fax: 973-458-5289

Library of Congress Control Number: 2009930480

International Standard Book Number: 978-1-934813-08-9
Cover Illustration by Michael Morgenstern
Cover design by David Lemanowicz
Interior design by David Lemanowicz

Printed in the United States of America
10 9 8 7 6 5 4 3 2 1

First Edition

11 09

SHATTERED

I'm deep into practicing the cadenza of Mendelssohn's Concerto, playing the solo from inside the notes, bouncing, becoming them, lifting off the string. I'm blending with the recording. The music's rising from the living room. It fills up the house. The force of it carries me. I keep even legato bows and follow the stepping-stone notes. Pure radiant tone whispers the wings of a goddess. Step—skip—leap. Violin Girl.

The doorbell trips my rhythm.

I expect to see Winnie at the door, and start to say, "C'mon in," but I stop, startled. Out of a shadow, an old man clears his throat. He steps forward.

I get scared and push the door closed.

He puts his hand up, blocking the door from shutting. "Cassie?" The voice is Dad's, except it's worn, unsteady.

"Grandpa?" I open the door for him.

He walks in and leans toward me, too close. "I give you a Parisian violin and you forget." He's half-smiling, like he wants to be angry with me.

"I didn't forget," I say, nodding my head. "I was expecting Winnie—my friend."

"Are you ready for your solo?" He unbuttons his overcoat.

"You're coming to my concert?"

He straightens the knot of his tie. "That a problem?" He looks at me.

"No, no. Not at all. I'm just surprised," I say, smiling at him. "It's nice."

I start to turn away, to go get Mom and Dad, but I stop because the last time Grandpa was here, he brought me the vintage violin and Dad blew up, burst out the door, furious, without even speaking to him.

I look back at Grandpa and his patience is ticking, running out. And the longer I linger, watching his eyes, he seems sort of sad.

"What the hell are you doing here?" Dad abruptly stops beside me. He glares at Grandpa.

I step closer to the old man, who is a little shorter than Dad. I want to reach out to him because I love the Mangenot violin he gave me, and I can't bear to see Dad being so cruel to him. But I don't. I don't want to pick sides. So I stand there, stuck, wishing I could bolt to my room and hide.

"Frank." Grandpa nods. "Jeannine was right—to break the silence." He points at Dad, but keeps his finger close to his chest. "You had no right—keeping Cassie's solo from me."

Dad turns toward the steps. "Jeannine!" He sounds like I used to, when my big brother picked on me.

Mom marches down the steps. Her heels tap in staccato on the wooden hallway. "Hi." She extends her hand to shake Grandpa's, but instead, he leans over and kisses her on the cheek. "I'm glad you could make it," she says.

"You should've told me, Jeannine," Dad says, like Grandpa's not in the room.

"I wanted to surprise Cassie." She stands up straight and with a slight tilt of her head, looks at me and smiles.

What was she thinking, inviting him? He and Dad haven't talked in years. Why did she have to do this tonight, of all nights? Did she really think they'd get along? That this would be a *fabulous* surprise?

"If I'd known about this," Dad says to Grandpa, "you wouldn't have made the trip for nothing."

Mom's cheeks are red, but she's got her "in charge" smile on her face. "Frank, it's okay."

"No, it's not okay." Dad walks toward the door, opens it, and looks at Grandpa. Cold November air pours in. "I want you out of my house. Now."

"Frank, it doesn't have to be this way." Mom goes over to Dad and touches his shoulder.

Grandpa stands tall, but his head wiggles as he says, "It's not up to you, son."

"Why'd you come, Dad?"

It shocks me, the way Dad's not letting up on his meanness to Grandpa.

"To hear my granddaughter's solo debut." Grandpa turns and nods at me.

Dad tightens his hold on the doorknob. "Are you sure it wasn't to see her screw up?"

I shiver. Why's he taking this out on me?

9

"Frank." Mom tries to shut the door, but Dad won't let go. "Please. This is Cassie's big night. Let's keep the peace—for one evening."

Dad stares down at the ground. I rub my arms to chase away the goose bumps.

"Frank," Grandpa heads toward the door. "I'm attending this concert."

"Wait, I've got your ticket." Mom avoids Dad's reddened face when she passes him on her way to the kitchen.

Dad slams the door shut and leaves the room.

I look over at Grandpa.

He winks.

Dad speeds us to the concert in Mom's Mercedes. Cool air seeps into my new black heels, brushes my ankles and rises to my knees. When Winnie's teeth start to chatter, I remind my parents to turn on the heat. They haven't said anything to each other or to me, not even a hello to Winnie when she showed up as Grandpa was walking out to his car. I'm dying to talk to her about this mess, but not with them around. I jump out when Dad pulls up in front of Orchestra Hall.

Winnie takes her cello from the trunk. When I slam it shut, she asks, "What's going on?"

It's hard to find the words to answer her, since my brain is still trembling from Mom's surprise.

Winnie, carrying the cello on her back, as usual struggles to keep up with me. "Are you okay?"

I check my watch, then hold the door open for her.

"This way." Instead of going backstage, she heads toward our "dressing room." We discovered it when we went wandering around, exploring during a rehearsal break last year. Down the hall, just off the lobby, the small room we'd found is not much bigger than a closet. It has a mirror and a tiny restroom. Winnie smiles at me when she turns the knob and the door opens. It's locked sometimes, but not today. She switches on a light, leans her cello against the ledge below the mirror, and then I pull the door shut behind me.

The silence forces me to exhale. "My mom surprise-invited my grandfather to our concert." I hug my violin case to my chest.

"And this is bad because—?"

"My dad hates him."

"Why'd your mom invite your grandfather if your dad hates him?"

"Because he's the one who gave me this." I hold up my violin case. "When I was eleven."

"Oh. I didn't know that."

"And he's so excited to hear me play my solo. It's kind of sweet. But what if I screw up?"

"Don't go there."

"What if Dad loses it in the middle of the concert and starts a fight?"

"Would he do that?"

Good question. Who knows? Last week while I was practicing, he smashed a hole in his computer screen. And I still don't know why. So I don't know if he'll hold it together during my concert. I set down my case, catch a sideways glance at my hair, and am glad my up-do is holding. With jittery hands, I turn Mom's pearl-and-diamond earrings; preoccupied, I'm lost in the mirror, not really checking if the diamond is actually centered below the pearl.

"What is it?" Winnie stands on her tiptoes and leans into the mirror to touch up her lip gloss.

"I was so ready for this solo, and now—I'm not so sure."

Winnie swishes her ringlets into place. "Remember what Miss Sinclair always says."

"What do you mean?"

"You know—'Players have to be present to win.'"

"Easier said than done." I grab my violin case. "It's time to go."

I hold the starting pose and savor the feel of the Mangenot in my hand. Its deep cherry varnish shines in this room that's as quiet as moonlight. My heart beats the silent flap of butterfly wings. Then the conductor cues, and I move, lift, shift into the chord, slide and chop. Over rocky terrain I bounce and balance, tiptoe, tap, even out, sustain. Each and every note must count.

I falter.

I miss the slightest beat. Lose a breath.

Back in, I chop, cross over to the A string. Fingers flutter. Sense the note, steady back and forth, forth and back, accent it.

When the tempo slows, I catch Miss Sinclair's eye—she's in the first row, nodding her head, silently analyzing each passage—and she smiles, just after the octave passage. I keep the tempo. My fingers fly while I hold my violin steady, bowing, flowing.

I look up to see Dad's stare. He's a few rows behind Miss Sinclair. Frozen. He's here, but not here. I hold my position so the notes, the words, will say what Mendelssohn meant them to say.

My grandfather, on the other side of Mom, sits up straight, listens with his eyes closed, knowing the notes. Notes made of clay; I'm shaping them, sculpting them, trying to curve them at just the right pitch. Saying what I need them to say. A song without words that says everything. A crystal held up, heavy and delicate, refracting light, a prism glimmering light.

Backstage is already in party mode. Winnie runs over to me, screaming my name, squealing, reaching up to hug me big, swaying me from side to side. "You did it, girl!"

I don't know why I start to cry. She's listened to all my fears through tryouts, and complaints after lessons, and dreams at performance breaks. She's kept me going and knows what this solo means to me.

"You can't cry. It's party time!"

We get our things and head over to the reception. I feel like there's luminous light shining down, and I'm floating goddesslike in its path.

In the hallway we run into our conductor, "Anal Al." "Nice work, Cassie." He reaches out and shakes my hand.

"Sorry about the beginning, missing that beat."

"Don't sweat it." Walking away, he says, "It'll come."

"I'll look at it again."

He turns around and smiles. "First, go celebrate."

Mom surprises me at the entrance with a bouquet of purple roses. Soloists usually get flowers, but I thought she'd be too busy to deal with getting me some. As I inhale the sweet floral scent, the room's becoming crowded. Mom's shoulders are touching mine, and it's the closest I've been to her in ages.

Grandpa leans over and kisses me on the cheek. "You make me very proud."

"Thank you."

He's smiling and calm, like something wrong is now right.

"The Mangenot—it's special." I smile at him.

"Exquisite."

Miss Sinclair puts her hands on my shoulders and says, "Cassie, my dear, you were wonderful. You played beautifully, and the effect was stunning." Her braids flop around her head as she nods, accenting her words.

"Thank you."

"It was your best solo yet."

"Even with that missed beat?"

"Even with that." She envelops me in a hug and her lilac-scented perfume. The brocade of her red jacket shimmers when I return her hug. Then she turns to Mom and congratulates her.

Winnie's parents come over. Mrs. Williams pulls me into a hug and holds on. "I'm so proud of you." Her dad practically dislocates my shoulder from shaking my hand with such enthusiasm. Winnie rolls her eyes. They're so free and open; next to them, Mom looks especially tense in her black crepe suit, as if she's wondering why they're hanging around.

I've often dreamed about Winnie's parents adopting me. They're so easy to talk to. But Mom's discomfort with them comes out in fragments of responses—like they're not worth whole sentences. She once told me that they remind her of unmatched hippie twins, since Win's mom has a Sixties-era hairstyle and is a typical Swedish blond. Her African American dad still has an Afro, and tonight, they're wearing their usual thrift shop outfits. Mom thinks they're strange.

I introduce everyone to my grandfather, and Winnie's parents take turns asking him a lot of questions about himself, as if it's perfectly normal that he's here. Miss Sinclair gives him lots of attention, too, and Mom starts to relax.

In the center of all these people, I only half listen to their conversation because I'm watching Dad, who's not part of our circle. He's off to the side, standing by himself, leaning against the door with his arms crossed. Usually he's friendly to Winnie's parents and cordial to Miss Sinclair, but as long as my grandfather's here, I know he's going to keep his distance. He's ruining my party mood, standing there like he's a security guard. I want him to mingle like all the other parents or at least go get some punch.

When her parents go over to talk to him, Winnie invites me to ride home with her later. That's when I shift into celebration mode. "Let's get some punch."

Winnie links her arm in mine. One of our friend's, Rosa, who plays the flute, is taking pictures. Winnie wants one of the two of us, but first she poofs out her frizzy reddish hair before we pose. Being taller than Winnie, I lean my head on top of hers and we laugh when the flash blurs our vision.

Winnie invites Rosa, Ariel, and Tamika to join us. They dissect all the parts of my solo, but I only hear snippets of their conversation:

"Accurate fingering."

"Very clean."

"It sounded fluid, not choppy."

". . . nice even notes."

"Perfect accents."

Their comments would be great captions for my scrapbook photos. For later. And other days.

I open the door into a war zone. Upstairs, Mom's yelling. "She was perfect tonight, and you said nothing."

I close the door gently behind me, and tiptoe to sit on the bottom step.

"What do you want from me?" Dad snaps back at her.

"How about, 'You were terrific.' It's that simple."

"How about—'you were incredible, and thanks for showing me up.'"

I wrap my arms around myself and hold on tight.

"You're not making sense."

"She gave the old man what he wanted. I sure never could."

Sharp pain pierces my stomach. I cross my arms and bend into it.

"So this is all about you—and not Cassie like it should be. You're being ridiculous, Frank."

"There you go, putting me down again."

"I want you to see our daughter for the brilliant violinist she's become."

I hear footsteps and scurry around the corner. I stand there, still as a statue.

"No, Jeannine, you just want to remind me on a daily basis that I'm a worthless piece of shit."

CRASH. It sounds like the wall is caving in.

A door slams.

I quickly tiptoe down the hall to the bathroom, lean over the toilet and vomit. Then I sit on the toilet seat lid and pretend I'm invisible. When rapid footsteps pound down the steps in Dad's rhythm, I lean over and lock the door. He hurries past the bathroom. The back door slams. I sit there until my heartbeat slows to a rate that I can barely feel, and then I slip off my shoes and go up to my room.

At the top of the stairs, ripped wallpaper surrounds a hole marking the spot where Dad has just exploded.

Calliope, my cat, is a calico coil on top of my pillow. She lifts her head to look at me. I whisper her name and she nuzzles her head back into place.

I lie down with my head on the small part of the pillow she's left for me and curl myself up toward her. I don't care that I'm still in my coat. I pet Calliope's head and listen to her purr, each breath a note in a song that lulls me to sleep.

Winnie's invitation to go to lunch is perfect timing. I get ready faster than usual. Her sister gives us a ride and after we eat, we wander through the downtown shops. Around three, when Winnie says she has to study and practice, I really don't want to go home. But I have a lot of homework and need to practice, too, so I go home anyway.

Inside, the house is quiet. I don't bother telling Mom and Dad I'm home because it's peaceful and I don't want to jinx it. There's noise in the downstairs office, so Mom's probably working. Upstairs, Dad's office door is closed, so he's already taken cover. I avoid looking at the hole in the wall as I go to my room.

Calliope's in the middle of my unmade bed, sitting on top of my flannel pj's in her hen position. She's mellow, like she just finished meditating. I kneel down and lean over to pet her. She lifts her chin and I give her long white furry neck a few strokes with my knuckle.

I have a ton of homework to do, but I can't stop thinking about the part in my solo I messed up last night, so I get out the music and study it. Then I take out my violin, do some scales, and forge ahead with my solo.

I mess up again in the same spot. I play those few notes, up and back, back and forth, over and again, going slow. When the section is finally smooth, I start at the beginning of the piece.

This time, I'm in easy, over and through the difficult passage. I smile at how it felt just right this time. I go on, getting deeper, going inside, springing up into something higher. Calliope's at my feet. She nudges my ankle, then weaves in and out of my legs. She's hungry, but the Mangenot is magic. It carries me. I close my eyes and this is all there is. I soar somewhere new.

"Cass!" Dad shouts from downstairs. Cupboards slam, pans clang.

Calliope screeches a short, high-pitched meow. She's gone—oh no—she's down in the kitchen with Dad. I drop the bow on the bed, grip my violin and run down the stairs. "Yaaapp."

Dad grabs Calliope's neck. "Damn cat's whining at me." He yanks her by the collar, lets her hang in mid-air. "I don't have to listen to this." Her eyes are big, bulging; her head pulled to the side. He shakes her.

"Dad, give her to me." I set my violin on the table. "I'll feed her. Sorry."

He throws her.

Calliope shrieks. She lands turned around, motionless.

"I should've never let you keep it."

When I lean down to pick her up, I bump into Dad and he topples into the refrigerator.

He grabs my violin by the neck and heaves it. In slow motion, it hits the kitchen window, and resonates with a pathetic, deep percussive sound. Glass shatters into a flawless spider web as the wood splinters, opening the belly of the violin. The neck cracks. Strings vibrate, loud, and in the aftermath, they ring. It lands and collapses in on itself. My violin. The whole thing fits perfectly into the kitchen sink. I stare at it—at him, stunned.

"You're not my dad anymore."

He bristles. Towering over me, he rubs his nose with his knuckle. Then quickly, he moves toward me.

Mom appears, gets in between us. He stops. Mom's teary. I hold Calliope tight. She digs her back claws into my stomach as I open the door. Mom grabs my wrist and holds on. "Don't go." Her voice is shaky. "We'll work it out."

Her tears dissolve her disguise, and I see my real mother at last: a person who's been hiding scared in a made-up world of perfect clothes, perfect table settings, and a perfect job.

"You're too late!" I shake my arm free and shove past her. I run down the steps, two at a time.

The frosted air stuns my face. I keep running. Calliope's head bumps against my jaw. After I'm a block away, I turn to make sure Dad's not following me. When he isn't, I slow to walking. The swiftness of Calliope's heartbeat echoes off my own. I pet the thick fur at the top of her head, where it's black above her white nose, just below the patch of gold. Across the street, a car pulls up and honks. Calliope freaks. She digs her claws into my neck and wriggles free. She ripples through the path between the two houses.

"Calli— Come back—Calliope!"

I run after her. The tears burn my frozen cheeks. She turns into an alley, and at the next house, disappears behind a trashcan. When I get to it, she's gone. I call out her name, watching the darkness for any sign of movement. If I'd just fed her when she nudged me instead of being obsessed with my music, none of this would be happening.

I walk two blocks in the alley, then circle back around the front of the same houses. Calliope's nowhere to be found. My brain feels light—it's filling up with cotton. I keep walking, keep looking. I pull up the hood on my sweatshirt. My hands feel brittle when I shove them in my jean pockets. I wish I had my gloves. Miss Sinclair's always on me to protect my hands, but that doesn't matter now. Thanks to *him*, I'll never play the violin again.

At the busy intersection, I do a quick scan for his blue Jeep. Zooming cars make the wind more intense. A dull spasm spreads into an ache at the back of my head. Nausea rumbles in my stomach, but the feeling quickly passes. A cramp invades the space where the nausea was. It clamps down. I lean forward, giving in to its force.

What did I do? How could I have made such a mistake? Ever since the summer, when I was picked to be a soloist, he's been in a perpetual bad mood. In response, I developed a new radar system that clicked on the minute I entered the house. It told me just how gently to walk on the eggshells. I adopted a "whatever" mentality. If he said, "That cat was on the good couch today," I'd say, "I'll keep her in my room from now on." Whatever he was mad about, I took a breath, thought *Whatever*, and then told him what he wanted to hear. I said and did whatever it took to keep the peace. The system was working. At least it was until tonight.

After a few minutes of waiting for the traffic to pass, and wishing—that I could find Calliope, that I was warm, and that a nice dad would switch places with this evil one who breaks things—I cross the street.

Where is she? Maybe two years ago when she was a stray, before I rescued her from the alley, she could care for herself. But after living indoors with us all this time, she needs me. She doesn't know how to live on the street anymore. I start to cry again. I need her. This is too much. I feel like I have wounds everywhere.

Right then, I wonder if he's home yet. Usually after he goes postal—like he did last night when he punched the wall—he takes a drive to who knows where, and eventually returns. Then it's like he's moved the edge of the storm to the other side of the Illinois border, to somewhere like Wisconsin, and things go back to being normal. Well, as normal as they can be when you live with a volcano.

My ears sting from the chilly air. Thinking about home starts a quivering in my chest. It gets heavier, but I keep on walking. He never wanted me to play. He didn't try to stop me. Instead he just overlooked it and I got used to his lack of interest. I learned to simply ignore it.

Beside the school playground, the swings just hang there in the darkness, looking lonely, as if they miss the kids. I sit on one and start to sway. My feet pump harder now, and the swing is going higher and higher. The wind pulls off my hood and bites my ears, while my hair blows all around my head. It's the lightest I've felt in a really long time. And even though I'm not dressed for the cold, I keep swinging, just to have this feeling.

When I stop, I turn on my cell phone. The message icon flashes on. I call Dad. His stupid voice mail comes on.

"How could you do that?" I say, and then I hang up.

I punch in my code to check my messages. It's Mom: "Cassie, where are you? Call me. I'll come and pick you up. You know your dad will eventually calm down. Please come home."

Never. I'm never going back.

27

I disconnect and stare off, away and down the street. One foot in front of the other, I get off the swing and head toward the El. Everything is fuzzy. The cotton in my brain floats as I slowly figure out that it's not so bad, being free of my family. Away from Dad's bad moods and Mom's way of going through the motions while avoiding Dad. But then the cotton in my head dissolves, the clouds tear apart quickly, leaving me alone in a black sky. I shiver.

I think of Michael, my brother, away at Case Western Reserve University in Cleveland. He's lucky he escaped. I remember how he told me to follow the evasion plan when he left in August. His advice was to stay away from base camp as much as possible. Was he ever right!

Why are things always so silent on a chilly night? It's like the cold comes along and sucks all the energy out of everyone. No one can speak. No one sees anyone else, either. Lots of cars drive up and down the street, but they don't seem to see me.

When the Gap sign comes into view, I know the El station lies just beyond it. I'll need a few bucks for the train, so I calculate how much money I have in my jeans pocket. Between the change I have left after going out to lunch with Winnie and allowance money Mom has just given me, I have about sixty bucks.

My phone rings like crazy—it's Mom, probably trying to get me to come home—so I shut it off. I can't think with that noise stinging my mind. With every step, I hear her in my mind, telling me to "plan ahead if you want to succeed"—but the only plan I have is to get to Chicago, to Union Station. My brain is mangled up, crashed like my violin.

On the train I sit near the door. I've never gone into the city by myself this late in the evening. Especially not on a school night. I know I'm supposed to be alert to my surroundings, but the blurry passing of the dark night makes my mind drift. It starts to snow, and as we get closer to the city, the lights tint the sky silver.

The sudden silence jars me alert. "End of the line, miss."

I get off the El. "He doesn't even care about what happens to me."

"Excuse me?" asks the woman walking beside me.

"Nothing. It's nothing." I head in the opposite direction. *Look like you know where you're going.* I spot a small café and decide to get some hot chocolate. Then I'll sit and think, and come up with my next move.

The warmth of the hot chocolate tastes good, even though it's watered down. I turn on my phone. 9:37—not too late to call Winnie.

After four rings, she answers.

I try to talk, but sobs come out instead of words. I shift and face into the corner of the café, so nobody else can see me.

"Cass? What's wrong?"

My brain feels light—it's filling up with cotton again.

"I left you a voice mail. Where are you? I hear people."

"Don't ask."

"No really—my dad will come and get you."

"No." I try to stop crying and wipe my tears on my sleeve. "Please, just listen."

"Okay. You're mom's looking for you. What happened?"

I sniffle. "I'll tell you later, but could you please go by my yard and see if you can find Calliope?"

"She's lost?"

"Yeah." The tears start up again, but I manage to hold them back. "And don't give her to my parents, okay? Keep her at your house for me."

"Are you okay?"

"Yes. No." I shift to look out the door of the café. A few people walk by.

"Cass, you're scaring me. I've never heard you sound so upset. This isn't like you to take off by yourself at night. Please, let us come get you."

"I have to go."

"Just tell me—what happened?"

I feel like a balloon with too much air in it. "Oh . . . my dad . . . we had a fight." My words feel like they aren't coming out of me, but from some stranger in the room whose balloon just popped. "My violin's broken."

"What?"

I recoil and wrap up into myself. I want to deny what happened, but I can't. Not now. "I wish we were talking about someone else's family."

"I could break his neck," Winnie hisses.

"He was having a bad night." I feel a clutch in my stomach. "It was all my fault."

"He should be the one who's gone, Cass. Not you."

I hold my stomach as sharp pains flash from one side to the other. The muscles tangle up, until they're as tight as a figure-eight knot. I bend over from the pain.

"Sleep over tonight, Cass."

"I can't."

"Why?"

"It's humiliating." The tears start to flow. "My own dad."

"But we're best friends!"

"Please, please, just go and rescue Calliope."

I click off and hear this voice in my head—it's Miss Sinclair—"Breathe . . . breathe," and I begin to breathe in deeply while leaning over, exhaling slowly on the way up. After a few breaths, the knot in my stomach finally unties.

That's when I remember I have a violin lesson tomorrow, and I'm stunned. I can't exactly go, now that he's destroyed my violin. But how can I *not go*? Monday lessons with Miss Sinclair are my life.

And so is Calliope. Winnie will find her. But what if she doesn't?

I want to hold myself the way a mother cuddles her crying baby. *Don't cry, don't cry, it will be okay, shhhh, shhh.* If I give up the violin, maybe Dad will calm down. He'll start to love me again, like before the Mangenot.

But how can I do that? It's hard to picture my life without the violin. And even if I wanted to play, how would I get a new one? Especially one as special as the Mangenot? It all feels too big for my heart to hold: never getting to play my Mangenot ever again. Reality collapses in on me, just like my violin, lying in the sink like a big, broken dirty dish.

I'm spacing out. And for some reason, I drift into a really old memory:

Mom drives us home from the violin shop. Sitting in the backseat, right behind her, I slide the new case onto my lap and open it. It's my first, very own violin, all shiny, the color of chocolate and caramel mixed together.

"What kind of violin is it, again?" I ask.

"It's called an 'Artist,'" Mom says.

I start plucking at the strings, "Twink-le, twink-le, lit-tle s-tar." The sunny day is warm on my face, and I can see Mom smiling in the mirror. The strings are slippery as I try the tune again and again, until finally the melody smoothes out.

I can't wait to show Dad. When we get home, I run into the house. I get it out of the case and hold up my new violin, showing it to him and smiling like I'd won first prize.

It's a surprise, but he doesn't smile. Instead, he glares at Mom. I pretend not to notice and play my new piece. But before I finish, Dad takes Mom by the elbow and steers her into the living room, away from my concert. But I keep going. I play all the way to the end, and when I stop, I hear him say to Mom, "Don't you think we should've talked about this first?"

Mom smiles at him. "Oh, honey, it's not a big deal. She's only five, for heaven's sakes."

"It is a big deal. Dad used to say it's when you need to start, if you're going to be . . . if you're hoping someday to be a soloist."

That feels like such a long, blurry time ago. But this question is crystal clear: Why *didn't* Dad want me to play the violin? And why did Mom *want* me to play? All these years, I'd never thought about it much. I wanted to play, and I just kind of ignored the fact that Dad didn't care if I did. I push myself now to search my brain for the answers, but my mind comes up blank. I'm in blank space.

10

"Could you spare some change, miss?"

I look up into the eyes of a white guy about my dad's age, whose wrinkles are shaded in with black dirt. He smells sour. For a second, I don't know where I am. When I remember, I pull myself together and get up to leave the café. "No. Sorry."

"God bless you."

Right. I start walking and don't know my destination, but I decide to look for Amtrak's waiting area. When I find it, I sit down and watch the different people passing by, pulling their luggage. Being with them, and hearing the announcement of trains leaving for different cities, gives me the feeling that I'm going somewhere, too. It's comforting and I relax into my seat.

A noise startles me and I realize a really hot guy is sitting beside me. He's unwrapping a chocolate bar the same shade as his short hair. When he talks to me, he seems like he's about my brother's age. "Bad dream?" he asks.

"My whole life is a bad dream right now."

He offers me some candy.

I break off a piece of dark chocolate and hand the rest back to him. It tastes good.

"Nick Ortiz." He offers me his hand. "And you are?"

"Cassie Prochazka."

"What happened?"

I look around. There's lots of empty seats, so why did he choose the one right next to mine?

"Looks like I'm it, if you're up to talking." He pops a chocolate square into his mouth.

I fold my arms across my chest. "Why do you care?"

"You're stressed out and my train's an hour late." He shrugs. "Nothing else to do."

"No offense, but you need to get a life."

"No offense, but you're a wreck."

I push my sweatshirt hood off my head and smooth my hair. Usually Winnie's the one who talks about everything, not me. I keep everything inside. Except with my brother. I take a deep breath, and even though I can't believe it, I begin to tell a total stranger about the eruption at home. "Calliope—that's my cat—was meowing at my dad, who hates her. But she was just hungry."

He crumples the candy wrapper into a ball and slips it into his backpack. "Uh-huh."

"I was upstairs, playing—I'm a violinist in the Chicago Youth Symphony."

"So you're really into the violin?"

"Yeah, we just had a concert last night. I played a solo."

"How'd it go?"

"It was incredible."

"You were?"

"My teacher said it was my best performance."

"Cool."

"Yeah, so Dad yelled for me to get my cat out of the kitchen. When I got there, he was shaking her. I said I was sorry that she was annoying him—and told him to give her to me. And that's when he threw her."

Nick stops breathing and stares at me. "That's intense."

"This is embarrassing." I avoid his eyes.

"You think you're the only one with a crazy family?"

I shift to look into his eyes. "You, too?"

He smiles and beneath it, I sense he's been through some stuff. His brown eyes are so warm that for a minute they make me forget what I'm saying.

"Then what?"

"When I picked her up, I accidentally bumped him and he fell against the fridge."

"Go on."

"That's when he—he broke my violin."

Nick crosses his arms over his chest. He probably wishes he'd taken a different seat by now, one far away from me. Like at the other end of the station.

"I couldn't do anything except watch it go flying. And wait for it to hit."

"For real?"

I nod.

"So where was your mom?"

"Never in the right place at the right time, that's where Jeannine was."

"Jeannine?"

37

"My mom—but I'm not thinking of her in that way anymore. Not after tonight."

Nick waits.

I tell him the rest of the story. Then he says, "It's good you got out of there."

"I was trying to protect Calliope. But she got away from me right after I ran out of the house. And now she's in even more danger, because eventually she'll go home and I won't be there to protect her. But I can't go back."

"I don't know you, but I'm glad *you're* safe."

I'm choking on the tears that are coming. "If I'd fed her on time, Dad wouldn't have flipped out."

"Hey, hey."

"I should've fed her as soon as I got home around four. That's when she usually eats. I should've known."

I should've listened to Michael and stayed away from home base. Dad's been losing it, breaking things for a while now—and none of it mattered, but I couldn't let him hurt Calliope. And now my violin's gone, and so is my cat.

"Looks like your dad needs to buy you a new violin."

A current of sadness flows through me. Now I wish I hadn't told this really cute guy my horrible story. It seems to have drained the goddess beauty out of me. The truth makes me feel so ugly.

The announcement for the train departing to Iowa forces Nick to gather up his stuff. "Sorry to bail on you, but that's me."

"Whatever."

He puts on his jacket. "You're not waiting for a train, are you?"

"Yes."

"Look—you should really call someone—your best friend, a boyfriend—someone."

"I'll figure it out." I shift in my seat.

"What are you, fifteen, sixteen?"

"Fourteen."

"It's cold out. Do you even have a coat?"

"Don't worry."

"Here's my number." He yanks a pen out of his backpack and jots it down. "Just in case."

The kindness of his reaching out to me—a total stranger basket case—makes my tears come back.

He slips on his backpack. "Be careful, okay?"

I nod.

I watch him go and don't want him to leave. Which is ridiculous, because I don't even know him. He could be some psycho-killer. But there's something about him that tells me his sweetness is for real.

The faded-out clock face on the dirty wall is hard to read. When I squint, I can just make out that it's two minutes after midnight. It's hard to keep my eyes open any longer. I want to sleep for years.

I'm wearing my favorite outfit—the one I had in fourth grade—purple jeans with the purple stretchy top and the pretend diamonds in the shape of a butterfly. I get out my violin and start doing scales, but stop when I hear this loud sound. WHACK. WHACK. WHACK. I can't concentrate because it's hacking at my brain. I look out the window. Dad's chopping down the tree right outside my window. Grandpa's tree. WHACK. WHACK. WHACK.

I run outside and start yelling, "Stop! Stop!" but he can't hear me. "Stop! Don't hurt Grandpa's tree!" He goes on hacking, tearing off the branches, limb by limb. The big tree was once just a seed in Grandpa's hand. Twigs are flying, sawdust gets in my hair, covers my favorite shirt, burns when it gets in my eye. "Stop!" I cry, but he doesn't even look at me. It's as if I'm invisible.

I kneel down, crying, and smell the sweetness of the sawdust as I run my hands over the rings in the smooth stump. Then I fall over in a heap, wondering how I will ever tell Grandpa about his baby tree.

I wake up startled, thinking about my grandfather,

about his violin. I should tell him about the Mangenot, except that I hardly even know him. And why don't I know him? Yesterday was the first time I'd seen him since that day he showed up when I was eleven to give me his violin. In all these years, I haven't seen him. Not until Jeannine's big surprise, of inviting him to my solo.

Questions and more questions. They leave me so agitated. I want the answers. And then it's like the moon shifts in my mind and lets in a snippet of light. I rub my arms, feel their strength—muscles defined from practicing twenty-five hours a week—and I push myself to get up. Someone has some explaining to do. It's time the people in my family start talking; it's time someone gave me some answers.

That's when I know where I'm going. I'm going to Pretoria. To see my grandfather.

But first, I call Winnie. "Did you find her?"

"No." She sounds sleepy. "My whole family went with me, too. We split up into different search parties."

"Did you check my back porch, the front steps?"

"Yeah, and then Dad and I sat out front in the car for a while. Still no sign of her."

"What if she's in there? With him?"

"No one went in or came out. We were there about a half hour. Then I had to pee. I'm sorry, Cass."

"Win, what am I going to do?"

"Where are you?"

"Never mind. Do me a favor."

"I told you we'd come and get you."

"No, I need you to get me some information. Off the Web."

"Why?"

"Please, just look up this name, and get me the address."

"Hold on."

While she works on it, I get up and ask some guy if I can borrow a pen.

"Ready?"

"Yeah."

She gives me my grandfather's address and I write it below Nick's number.

"Thanks. Can you go back and look for Calliope tomorrow?"

"Oh, my God—you're going to Pretoria? Tonight?"

"Win, please, promise me you'll look for her!"

"Okay, okay, but call me a lot, okay?"

"I will. I promise."

The guilt and fear are starting up again, like music that cancels out the lyrics because the tone is too heavy. My chest starts trembling. I turn off my phone and slam it shut, disappointed that Winnie didn't find Calliope. But I make myself keep walking to the ticket office.

"No trains to Pretoria," says the clerk. "Have to take a bus to get there."

I start to ask the clerk about the bus when she says, "Out the main doors, cab stand is to the right. Bus station is about a mile away."

I thank her, and though I definitely need to sleep, having a destination has given me a burst of energy. I catch a cab, and in a few minutes I have a bus ticket and twenty dollars to spare. After I carefully wad up the cash and slip it into the pocket of my hoodie, I hurry outside, since the bus should be here any minute.

When it pulls up, I get on and it stinks, like someone just sprayed air freshener to cover the smell of sweaty people and cigarettes and dirty diapers. I hold my breath until I get to the second seat. Then I plop down and slide over. A chill seeps through the thin glass of the foggy window.

Right then, I miss my brother Michael and wish he were going with me. Before he left for college, I helped him get his stuff together for his dorm room. We made a lot of trips to the mall, and we had some good long talks. Nick sort of reminds me of Michael. Well, sort of. I'd never think of my brother as being hot.

Then I remember how much my grandfather wanted me to have that violin. And even though I don't want to have to tell him it's gone, someone has to tell him. For a second I consider not being the messenger, because I don't want to upset him.

I check my watch. It's almost three in the morning. I pass out until we arrive in Pretoria, sometime around six.

I wake up, grungy, in a wrinkled mood. When I get off the bus, my legs are stiff and my back is sore from sleeping in a cramped space. The dawn that's just about to crack open the sky is daunting. I tremble in the cool air and zip up my hoodie.

Inside the station it's hot—it feels like it's been closed up too long—and I suffocate from the smell of roasted cinnamon almonds. I use the washroom, and when I come out, and see the gray walls and the old architecture of the room, I suddenly don't want to be here. Only a few people are milling around, and they don't look like travelers. But they all look like I probably look: lost, alone, and hungry.

What *am* I doing *here?* I should be at home, just opening my eyes to my lavender bedroom, waking up to the poster of my idol, Joshua Bell. Then I should be getting dressed and walking into school, beaming about my solo. I should be sitting in first-period math beside Winnie, listening to Mr. Gold drone on and on, making "x's" and "y's" all over the board.

I know that it was only last night that I got on the El and rode out of Oak Park, but it feels like years ago. My heart cracks a little deeper when I realize that Calliope is out in the cold, somewhere all alone. Or even worse, home and being terrorized by Dad. I miss her. I want to talk to Michael so I turn on my cell, but he'd kill me for waking him up, so I change my mind about calling. The message icon is still on.

Dad didn't call back. All the messages are from Jeannine, about an hour apart:

"Cassie, please call me. *Now*."

"Winnie phoned. Where are you? I'll pick you up. We need to discuss a plan for damage control."

"Cassie, no need to be the victim. Come home! It's time to get tough and handle things."

She sounds like she does at work when she's troubleshooting a minor snag on one of her ad campaigns. Only this is our family that's falling apart. After her last message, I can't listen to her anymore and shut off the phone.

Tiredness seeps into me like someone has injected me with a sleeping serum. I drop to the hard wooden bench, lie down, clutch my cell phone, and fall asleep. I'm practically drinking in the sleep when I feel this tug at my side, followed by shouting.

"Wake up! Wake up!"

I wish they'd shut up, but then I realize they're yelling at me.

I open my eyes to see a dad-type guy chasing a kid my age. The door rattles when the handle snags his coat pocket.

"Are you all right?" asks a young woman wearing a man's parka over a cotton housedress.

I sit up, startled.

"I tried to wake you. He was yanking the cash out of your pocket just as I came in. You were catching some serious Z's."

I reach inside my pocket. It's empty. I'm frantic now, as I search my other pocket. But nothing's there, either. I want to punch her ugly black glasses, but my violin is hitting the window and the image of being as rotten as my dad keeps me from doing anything so stupid.

I'm outside myself, watching as I talk to this strange woman and the guy who tried to chase down the thief.

"Sorry." He puts his hands in his pockets. "He got away—he was too fast—way too fast for me."

"Thanks for trying." I look around, wondering what I'm going to do now, without any money left.

"Are you all right?" The strange woman's leaning over me, her pointy nose almost touching mine. Her eyes are an off shade of blue, and I resist the urge to back away from her face. Instead, I lean away.

"Fine. I'm fine." I'm talking myself into it so she'll go away.

"You should tell the attendant." She points over to the ticket booth. "She can get Security for you."

"That's okay."

"Security could call the cops."

"No cops."

She backs away from me like I hit her. "I come over here just about every morning after the shelter closes. The Security people are real nice."

"It'd probably be more trouble than it's worth," says the guy. "He's long gone by now."

"It's your life." She shrugs.

"I wish I had some change to spare, but I'm flat broke," says the guy, showing me his empty palms.

"Me too," says the woman. She points outside. "I'm probably gonna have to work the median strip to buy lunch."

"You should call your folks," he says, pointing at my cell phone. "It's rough out there on the streets."

So they're homeless. Pieces of thoughts start to swirl in my brain. All the events of the last ten hours are stalling out in my mind. I feel this current of fear about Calliope, twisting up with a strand of hopelessness about being broke, all of them winding up tight in my mind. That's when I rewrite it in my head: *They* are *homeless*. I am *away* from home. It sort of helps, and then I take a breath. When I exhale, I hear a violin playing and I turn my head in that direction.

"Hey, thanks, but I have to go." I get up and follow the music. It gets louder and louder as I walk through the bus station toward the entrance, through the revolving door, and outside.

I recognize it right away. The Dixie Chicks tune, "Let Him Fly." Winnie and I know the words to all their songs. A man wearing a military jacket with long, stringy gray hair is standing there, his open violin case at his feet. It's jarring to see such a big guy playing a slow song on a violin, which looks like a toy in his hands. But in a few seconds, I'm in the sadness of the melody. "I'm gonna let him fly,

fly." And I think about my dad, and I think about my violin flying. Everything flying away. I'm somewhere between the silent echoes of the bass and treble of that violin and the words "Oh, I'm gonna let him fly." And this time, when he plays the notes for the word "fly," it comes out in a whisper and I know that whisper. It's barely there, yet weighted. Breathing.

He finishes and I clap.

He nods at me, looks away, then back at me. He's expecting me to put money where my praise is, but I have nothing.

I should move on, but I can't. "Could I play it?"

"No." He puts his hand out like he wants me to back off.

I step forward. "C'mon, please?" I point at his violin. "Just one song."

"Uh, well." He looks me up and down. "I guess you don't look like the type to run off with Mildred here."

"My three-quarter size was named Hermione. You know—Harry Potter?"

"Oh yeah."

"I love those books."

He pats his violin. "She's named after my first love."

I point at it again. "So, will you let me play it?"

"You know how?"

I nod. "I've been taking lessons since I was five."

"Be gentle with the girl," he says, handing me the violin, then the bow.

I take his violin and tuck it under my chin. It's not the fit I'm used to, but once I get into a starting pose, something clicks. Like my brain has just recognized my violinist self. I stand tall, imagining Anal Al giving the downbeat, and then I shift into playing my solo.

When I get tripped up in the same place I did at my concert, I stop.

"Keep going," he says.

After a few notes, it's like I'm inside the soul of this amazing violin goddess. I've left the earth, left my family, left Winnie, left Miss Sinclair, even left Calliope. I'm out there, birthed free of all the pain, and I'm my right self. A bird soaring, breathing, flapping over notes, flying free, no boundaries, wrapping one note into another, until I'm enveloped in silk, beautiful purple silk, wings flapping silk in the free breeze of blueness, a refuge.

People are clapping and whistling. I guess while I was flying, a crowd had formed around me. The owner of the violin starts to clap then, too, and he's smiling, and he's not a scary marine man anymore. He looks like a really nice guy. The people walk by us and drop coins into his case, a few dollar bills, and one guy drops in a five.

"Hey, we could buy breakfast," I say, smiling.

He puts his hands on his hips. "You think I'm gonna give you a cut?"

"Would be nice." I hand him back his violin. "I just got robbed."

"I guess I could do that. McDonald's is right around the corner." He points down the street.

I turn toward that direction. "Let's go."

"You sure are a friendly chick." He's staring into my eyes with a big grin on his face.

I'm a hungry chick is what I'm thinking, but his eyes are kind of beady and he's suddenly creeping me out. "Whatever."

He squats and picks up all the money and puts it in his big coat pocket. This annoys me, since I earned most of it, but I don't say anything because I don't want him to change his mind about treating me to McDonald's.

He packs up his violin and leads me around the corner. The big golden arches call to me. I zip my sweatshirt and put up the hood.

"What's your name?"

"Cassie."

"I'm Harley." He opens the door to McDonald's for me and I feel like I'm going to dine at the Drake in downtown Chicago or something. That's how happy I am to be here. All the smells mixed up together—salty fries, sausage, grease, and coffee—they make me smile for the first time since I left home.

I've never had coffee before, but this seems like a day to start drinking it. My first sip and it singes my tongue and the taste is a jolt of liquid dirt. Why does everyone rave about it? I take off the lid and decide to let it cool while I devour my sausage, egg, and cheese McMuffin. I'm halfway through it when I remember I'm with someone and look over at Harley.

"Long night?" he asks.

His question feels a bit too close and I don't answer right away. Instead, I picture myself as a cartoon character with a lightbulb in the bubble and decide to invent myself. "Yeah, my grandfather's really sick and my folks are out of town, so I hopped the first bus from Chicago. Not fun—a bus in the middle of the night."

"Can't say it's on my list of things to do before I die." He pops a stray biscuit crumb from the table into his mouth.

"My grandfather gave me my first violin, so, you know."

"Where in Pretoria?" He sips his coffee.

"That's the thing—I don't know." I look out the window.

He pounds on the table. "You're pullin' my leg."

"No—I mean, I have the address, but I don't know where it is from here." I show him the piece of paper with my grandfather's information.

He grabs it from me. "Okay, okay, you had me going there for a minute."

"You live here?"

"Barely."

"What's that supposed to mean?" I clasp my hands and rest them on the table.

"I'm a veteran. Contrary to popular belief, our beloved government doesn't take care of its own."

"Which war?"

"Ah, you're a sweetheart." He lifts his coffee cup to me. "Hats off to you for not assumin' I'm an old man. Seriously, I served in Nam back in '67. Right out of high school."

"Wow."

"Yeah. I'm old enough to be your father. Speaking of which—yours really let you take a bus in the middle of the night?"

"Uh, no, it was a quick decision. Like I said, my folks are out of town and I got the call that my grandfather's sick." I crumple up my wrapper and offer my coffee to Harley. "I really should get going."

"How you going to get there? It's pretty far."

I cross my arms and hold on tight. No money and no direction and I'm not sure about Harley. I was hoping to be on my own after breakfast. "Would you help me earn cab fare?"

"It's your lucky day. My car's just down the block." He stands up. "I'll give you a lift."

"Wait! You know, I'll save you the bother." I pull out my cell. "I'll see if one of my grandfather's neighbors can come get me." It amazes me how once you start lying, it's really pretty easy to keep lying.

It rings, rings, rings. *Please Grandpa, answer your phone*. Harley paces a few steps, back and forth. I let it ring five more times and an answering machine never picks up. It rings and rings. I look up at Harley.

He stops pacing. "We're on?"

"You don't mind giving me a ride?" I slowly inch out of the seat.

"Not at all." He heads for the door.

I'm not sure about it being a good idea, but I go with him anyway. I'm walking past boarded-up storefronts and almost trip over the trash strewn all over the sidewalk. I'm wondering why I'm not only talking to a stranger, but actually going to get into his car. Every grown-up I have ever known is yelling really loud in my head: *DON'T GO!*

His car turns out to be a yellow really old VW bug. He opens the door for me and the stench of stale cigarette smoke wafts over me. Inside, it's like a garbage can—wrappers, an apple core on the dash, and empty soft drink cans everywhere. "Ready?" He puts his hand on my shoulder and creeps me out again, the way he's acting like we're on a date. Fear chases its way up my spine, but I don't have time to be scared. I have to think.

I duck out of his grasp and take off like I'm athletic, which I'm not.

"Hey, come back here! The party's just gettin' started!"

Into high gear, I run like I'm trying out for the Olympics. Harley chases me. I run, and hope I'm heading into an area where there's a gas station or shops, restaurants, and people. I'm pumping my arms and kicking my legs, but he gains on me and yanks a handful of my hair. Tiny pin pricks of pain sound off all over my head and it hurts so much, it blinds me and I trip. I open my eyes just in time to right myself and get away. I will my legs to go faster. He grabs my hood this time and the zipper is cutting into my neck, choking me. I'm trying to unzip it but he's pulling too hard. I can't get away and he's reeling me in by the hood. He puts one of his fat gross arms around my waist and I attack his wrist with my nails and bite hard at his shoulder.

"Bitch!"

He wrenches out his arm and I take off again. After what feels like a five-hundred-yard dash, I turn around to check on him and he's down, leaning against a building on the corner, rubbing his arm. I keep going, running as fast as I can. My head aches and the pain in my side is intense, but it's not as bad as what could happen if he catches me, so I run through the agony.

The sound of traffic up ahead makes me run even faster. The huge light swaying green in the middle of a busy intersection makes me cry. I can see a convenience store just up ahead, and I don't slow down for fear of Harley getting into his car to come after me.

I don't recognize myself. I'm locked in the restroom, inside the convenience store, looking in the mirror. I'm breathing hard. I'm bug-eyed. My cheeks are red and there's some dirt on my forehead. My hair's all tangled and there're red welts on my neck from where the zipper cut into it. "Oh, my God." I remember myself dressed for my concert in the black silk dress with skinny straps and the satin bolero jacket. *Now I've become a runaway.*

Freaking out, I close my eyes. I call to the goddess—the one I felt while I was playing Harley's violin—the one who helps me play so well. As I call her, I try to visualize the white, gauzy, divine-kind-of-presence inside myself. I remember the sense of flying free. And she's there—I feel her there, the strong, winged being who is wrapping note into note.

I open my eyes, but the goddess has slipped away. Splashing water on my face, I tell myself I need to find her. My problems are way too big right now and I need help. I need guidance and I'll take it from wherever I can get it. I hope she'll help me figure things out, and help me find my way. I brush my hair with my hand, gently rubbing my head and smoothing out the tangles with my fingers. It shocks me when I remember that it's Monday for the rest of the world. Normally, I have violin lessons on Mondays. But who knows if my life will ever get back to normal?

I turn my phone on and discover that it's 11:45—too early to call Winnie to check on Calliope—she'll still be in school. My lesson isn't until 3:30, and even though I won't be able to make it, at least I can call, be responsible and cancel. I see that there're twelve voice mail messages waiting, probably all from Mom. I punch in Miss Sinclair's number.

She's not home. I leave a message, shut the phone off, and start to cry. I don't want to miss my lesson. I've never not practiced every day. I don't want to be hiding in a restroom out in the middle of nowhere. A knock on the door and a woman's voice prompts me to get moving. I carefully open the door, and when I see it's not Harley, I walk out. I stand off to the side of the counter, feeling comforted by the clerk's presence. Watching the door, I call my grandpa.

It rings and rings and rings some more. Even the rings sound empty, and I finally give up and accept that he's not home.

I walk out and lean against the store, watching for Harley. I guess if he isn't here by now, he gave up on me. That's my hope, but I watch for him anyway. The cold bricks cut into my back and it starts to sink in that I'm in need of a Plan B. For the first time that day, some patches of blue take back the sky. It's still chilly, but the sun slips out from between a crack in the clouds and warms my face.

A car drives by and brown leaves swirl in its wake. If I were living an entirely different life, I would be thinking this is a beautiful day.

Since there's nothing to do, I listen to my messages.

"Call me." This one's from Mom in the middle of the night. She sounds tired, and she's not wasting precious energy saying anything that's not necessary.

The second one is from her, too, at six in the morning. "Cassie, stop this nonsense. Now. Call me!"

An hour later, she called again: "Cassie, stop being a drama queen. Call me! Or better yet, come home. Now."

The next one is from Winnie: "Cass, I'm worried about you! Call me. Just tell me you're okay, please? Oh yeah, I went by your house before school today. No sign of Calliope. Sorry."

Calliope's the one I go to when Dad makes Mom mad, which usually turns into a fight. He ends up leaving and she holes up in her office. Right now, everything would be okay if I could just hold Calliope in my arms and kiss her little cat head.

The fifth message is from my brother: "Cass, where are you? Give me a call."

Mom again: "In about six hours the police will allow me to file a missing person's report. Please, Cassie. Don't put me in the position to have to do this. Call me."

After that, it's Miss Sinclair: "Don't think that just because you had such a great concert, that you can take today off. No, no, no, missy! Call me as soon as you get this." For some reason, her strictness makes me smile, and I wipe my tears. I can't listen to the rest, not if I'm going to keep going. Before I shut off my phone, I dig out the piece of paper from my jeans pocket and call Nick. I know it's crazy, because he'll probably be in school, but I call anyway.

He doesn't answer. I listen to his entire voice mail message for the strands of kindness in his voice. And I like the attitude that's coming through, too. Then I hang up without leaving a message, knowing I have to get in line to ask the cashier for help.

When it's my turn, I look around to make sure it's just me and the cashier. "Excuse me, sir."

"What's up?"

"I need help."

"You got money and want to buy somethin'?"

"Uh, no."

"Then I can't help you."

"But—"

"You kids always want somethin' for nothin'." He points at the door. "Go on. I have a business to run."

He's not even looking at me when he says this so he doesn't notice when I leave the store. Outside again, I pull up my hood. To my right, the phone book's dangling out of the booth. When I get in front of it, thinking I'll check it for information on shelters, the cashier opens the door, and shouts, "No loitering!"

His voice makes me jump. I'm not sure what to do next, or where to go, but I head out through the parking lot. The other side of the street is sunny, so I cross over to keep warm.

I stand there and look up and down the street. I could go back to the bus station and hang out, but Harley might still be there. So I decide to walk in the opposite direction, looking for a phone booth, or another convenience store, or a nice person.

I walk blocks upon blocks, passing all kinds of businesses. A dry cleaner, an insurance agency, a nail salon, a place that does African braids. My stomach growls like I never ate breakfast, and I'm long overdue for lunch. A steady stream of traffic flows both ways. I watch for signs of my goddess. Everyone in the world seems to have a sense of direction, a feeling of purpose. Everyone except me.

Food looks different when you don't have any money to buy it. I walk around the store, picking up food, then putting it back. I can almost taste the Thanksgiving in the turkey sub, the sharp in the cheddar. I'm dying for a huge gulp of juice, to feel the cool silkiness of it going down my throat. Passing the racks of chocolate bars makes me wish for the sweet smoothness of each square.

I take another lap, warming up, and trying to get up the courage to talk to the cashier. But I never do.

Outside, I locate the phone booth at the far end of the store. So tired, I lean against the metal part of the booth. I slide the phone book, heavy, and balance it on the ledge below the phone. The wind rustles the pages, making it difficult to turn them. I finally get to the yellow pages section, but there's nothing listed under "Shelters." So I try "Homeless Shelters." There's nothing there, either. I start to get antsy and flip back to the white pages. What's listed there is a "Shelter for Battered Women." A gust of wind blows the pages out of my hand. When I get a hold of them again, my index finger lands on "St. Luke's Roman Catholic Church."

That could work. I memorize the number, then let the phone book dangle, and call on my cell.

It rings and rings. *Please answer*. I almost hang up when a woman says, "Hello?"

"I need to get to a shelter."

"You sound young. I could direct you to a teen shelter."

"Great."

"Where are you now?"

I don't answer her, because I don't know. "Hold on, okay?"

Inside the store, I take a chance on the cashier, asking for the address of the store. He rattles off the address without yelling at me, but he doesn't look up from his cash register, either.

I go back outside and tell the woman where I am.

"There's one close to there. Hannah's House."

"Where?"

"About three miles. Just keep walking south. Make a left at Ridley Avenue. Go one block. Turn right on School. Then one more block, at the corner of School and Berry Streets."

I repeat it back to her to make sure I've got it.

"Yep."

"Thanks."

"No problem."

Three miles? I sit down on the curb. I'm not sure I can do it. The longest I've ever run in gym is one mile. But what choice do I have? I try to call my grandfather again, but he's still not there. So after about fifteen minutes, I ask the cashier to point me south and I start walking.

I try to remember how long it took me to run a mile in gym. About fifteen minutes? I do the math, figuring it will take me a little longer to walk it. Give or take, it could take me maybe a little over an hour to get to the shelter. In this weather, it sounds like eternity. I check the clock on my cell: 2:02. *Okay*, I tell myself. *By 3:30, you'll be somewhere.*

I wrap my arms across my chest and will myself not to think about the cold. My stomach growls and I tell myself food thoughts are also off-limits. To distract myself, I decide to do the alphabet game that we played on a road trip once. I find an "a" right away on a sign for a catering company and immediately start searching for a "b." The entire alphabet keeps me busy for about a half hour. I read each street sign along the way, even though I don't expect to see "Ridley" for a while.

The sky turns cloudy and the wind slows down. It's subtle, but I appreciate being able to walk without hugging myself. After a while I run into a Wendy's to use the restroom. Being warm for a change feels incredible. I take a long, really long drink of water from the fountain, trying to ignore the smell of juicy burgers. But I just can't avoid that delicious aroma, so I get out of there right away.

I walk and walk. For a second, I wonder if I'm really going the right way, so I stop. But I'm cold and tired, and the side of my right foot is killing me. I almost flip out just thinking I might not be going toward something. So I start walking again and focus on my breathing. It's only faint at first, then more audible; it has a strong goddess rhythm. I tell myself to believe that even if I can't see her, she's watching out for me.

At 3:37, the sun's streaking the sky with hazy clouds, and I panic once again. There's still no sign of Ridley Avenue. I decide to go two more blocks and if I don't see it then, I'll ask someone. I walk a long block, then a short one. But it's still not Ridley. When I see a woman come out of the dry cleaners, I run to catch up to her. She watches me closely. Even after I ask her about Ridley Avenue, she seems suspicious of me and keeps her distance. She points south, "I think it's two blocks from here."

I go there fast. When I see it, Ridley Avenue, I speed up, cross it, and then go left. After another long block, I smile again when I see School Street. I turn right and before I know it, I see Berry. On the corner is a large white Victorian with blue paint chipping off the trim. I'm out of breath, climbing the steps to the porch, but I'm so glad I finally made it to "Hannah's House." You'd think I was actually home.

The old wooden door is locked. I read the posted sign and discover they don't open until five. It's only 4:15, so I sit back down on the step and rub my arms when I start to shiver. I try to call my grandfather again, and I swear I can tell by the sound of the ringing that he's still not home. And he's not.

"Okay, Jeannine. Get ready to make your missing persons report, because I'm going in."

Just then, two girls turn the corner and walk my way. One looks like a mix between Winnie and our friend Ariel—she has Winnie's curls and Ariel's face. She says, "New blood." She looks and sounds like she's in college. "You joining the party?"

"Excuse me?" I ask.

"Must be her first night. She still has manners," the Asian girl says, then they look at each other and laugh like I'm not here.

"I'm from Oak Park—near Chicago."

They stop laughing and stare at me. The Winnie-Ariel girl asks, "What's your name?"

"Cassie."

"I'm Rachel," she says. She points with her thumb at her friend, and says, "This is Jessica."

The door behind us opens and an older woman appears. "You here to check in?"

We look at each other. "Yeah," says Rachel.

I follow them inside and sign in after them, even though I was here first. I don't mind. It should calm me down to watch them go through the check-in procedure, but my heartbeat speeds up again. I'm relieved to be here and scared to be here. Even though I'm feeling weird it must not show. The woman at the desk isn't put off—she's not dialing 911—and I guess I'm probably not having a heart attack, either.

She talks real slow and walks me through the forms. Then she tells me about the schedule for the evening: dinner, bed assignments, showers, snack. As she's saying, "Lights out at eleven," three more girls my age get in line behind me. She speeds up while reviewing a few rules. Then she asks if I'd like to plug in my cell phone. I nod. She points to a bin on her desk, and I choose the phone charger that matches my cell.

The floor creaks as I walk down the hall past different rooms as I head for dinner. There's a homey feeling to the old house, plus a funky smell. Kind of like the combo of beef stew and locker room. In the kitchen, off to the side of the cooking space, two picnic tables are jammed into the room. I spot several available outlets above a counter, so I connect my cell phone to the charger, and then plug it in. I hesitate before leaving it there. I'd be totally lost without it. I end up sitting down facing the phone so that I can keep an eye on it, and I'm across from Jessica and beside Rachel. Jessica hands me the bread basket and I join them in buttering a slice. As I bite into it, Rachel puts three pieces of bread into a napkin on her lap, folds them up, then slips them into her jacket pocket. I look over at Jessica and she smiles at me. I smile back, thinking she doesn't look at all like a homeless person. Instead, she looks like someone who'd fit in at my high school, or who could be sitting in my violin section.

Other girls come in and sit at our table, but I don't have the energy to be friendly. I'm weary from being cold all day, and my feet are burning sore. Right now, I just want to get through the night. One woman sets a bowl of soup at each place, while another sets out a large bowl of fruit. Jessica and Rachel talk about their day, spent wandering through different grocery stores. The rest of us just listen. No one adds anything. I eat more than usual, and put an apple into the pocket of my hoodie—for later. I don't even want to think about where I'll be tomorrow.

A woman tells us it's time to get our sleeping assignments. I grab my cell, then follow her upstairs. She leads us into a large white room with cots everywhere. The room smells of clean linens and old wood, but it's sort of musty, too. She moves from cot to cot, yelling out names and pointing to beds.

My cot is on the far side of the room, underneath a window. Jessica's is near the door and she lies down on hers. Rachel sits on hers, beside Jessica's, and they talk back and forth. They look like they're best friends. Watching them makes me miss Winnie.

Then I sort of lean down and half-sit on my cot as I look out the window, the blue blanket scratchy on my hand. It's already dark outside. Compared to my lavender bedroom, this room is nearly lifeless. It surprises me when my mind creates a picture of my room at home, like it wants me to remember every detail. The silver lavender bedspread and the matching silk curtains Jeannine wrapped dramatically around the rod. The French country pine desk underneath the window that goes with my bed, nightstand, and dresser. Jeannine wanted it decorated like a fancy hotel room, and it made me mad that she didn't care about what I wanted. At least she gave in on the Joshua Bell poster, but only if I framed it. Winnie says it's nice, but it still hurts that my room is more about Jeannine than about me.

Then I do what I always do when I'm upset. I stand up to get my violin out of the case, but then I sit down again fast, remembering—it's gone. I hold on to myself and lean over to stop from fainting.

"Okay, ladies. Now that you all have beds, it's shower time. I'll give each of you a number. Let's do this quickly and efficiently. Snacks in the lounge after your showers."

I'm dying for a shower, but wonder what's the point, since I have to put on the same dirty clothes. I lie on the cot to wait my turn, letting the big bedroom shrink and disappear. As I think about my broken violin, I'm in a darker shade of sad. My violin isn't the only thing broken; our family is, too. I turn over on my side, shut my eyes, and curl up.

Later, when my number's called, I walk through the maze of cots to the shower. It means a lot to me when I see the rack of clean scrubs waiting for us to wear to bed. There's no April Rain shower gel like Jeannine always gets for us. Sometimes I get so sick of that scent, but right now, I actually kind of miss her. There's barely a trickle of water, but the heat and the cleanliness seep into my skin, infusing me with a sense of hope. I wash with Ivory soap and lather my hair with Prell. Jeannine would call it all cheap stuff, but to me, it's luxurious just to get clean.

It's only nine, but it feels like the middle of the night. I'm sitting in the "family room," on a couch that feels like a wooden seat in a canoe. Rachel sits at the other end, and we're both in a kind of weary fog, staring at the TV. I couldn't tell you what we watched, and I bet neither could she. Then this commercial comes on for cat food. The cats are in a cat choir loft, singing "Chow, chow, chowwww." The third one from the left looks exactly like Calliope; I watch her for the entire commercial, and when it ends, I start to cry.

"I figured you'd break down sooner or later."

"What?"

"You've been the ice princess all night, like you don't have problems like the rest of us."

"Would I be here if I didn't have problems?"

"Exactly."

"I miss my cat, is all."

She scoots over and sits really close to me. "When you're homeless, it's the little things that get to you."

"Yeah. You know, I miss my cat more than I miss my parents."

"I love cats, too." She puts her arm around me. "It's gonna be okay."

I lay my head on her shoulder.

"You can't look at it as if your whole life's ahead of you, along with all your problems. Just think from day to day. Hell, sometimes I'm just living minute to minute."

I scoot closer to Rachel. She rests her head on top of mine. We don't talk, just stare at the TV, letting the images unfold without following the story. My breathing slows and I can't believe I am feeling peaceful at a homeless shelter, of all places. I surprise myself, letting a pure stranger hold me like this, but it feels good, and I actually feel safe. The quiet is perfect pitch.

Then her hand is on my boob, lightly then firmly. It startles me, but I don't move at first. She starts to press, gently moving her hand in a slow rhythm, upward and out. It's gross and I want her to stop.

I open my eyes. Without moving, I look out of the corner of my eye and see that Rachel's eyes are closed. I take her hand and put it on her lap. As I'm getting up, she says, "I should've gone slower. I scared you. I'm sorry."

"Don't ever do that to me, ever again!" I run out of the room through the hall and up the stairs.

Jessica's looking at me when I enter the bedroom. "Is Rachel downstairs?"

"Yeah." I avoid looking at her and just keep walking toward my bed. Under the stiff sheets, I turn to face the wall, and a chilly draft leaks through the window. My grandfather just has to be home tomorrow.

I need to talk to someone. Not Michael. Not Winnie. Definitely not Mom. It doesn't make sense, I know, but the person I really want to talk to is Nick. Go figure. It's ten and he's probably still up, so right then I call him.

"You all right?" he asks.

I turn over and realize some of the others are trying to sleep, so I scoot under the covers and whisper. "I'm in a shelter."

"Is it okay there?"

"Try YMCA inside a Victorian."

"It's better than the streets."

"True. But this day was weird. I mean, all day I tried to avoid thinking about being scared by looking for a goddess."

Nick chuckles. "I'd like to find a goddess myself."

"Not like that. I mean, like someone to watch over me, or something to hold on to, while things are bad."

"Oh, I get it. Like baseball."

"Baseball?"

"Life can suck, okay? But in baseball, there's always something that's awesome."

"What do you mean?"

"Like you might strike out and then the next at bat, get a hit, or an RBI—sometimes even a homer."

"Were you on your high school's team?"

"Still am. Made varsity as a sophomore last year."

"So you're a junior?"

"Too old for you?"

"No, I thought you were in college."

"Yeah, I get that a lot. The folks split suddenly. I grew up fast. Mom moved me to Iowa. Dad's still back in Chicago."

"I wish my dad would move out."

"Did you really just say that?" There's pain in his voice.

"I just can't take him anymore. How'd you handle it?"

"Like I said, I had to grow up fast. Baseball kept me going."

"If I was different—me and Dad—we might get along."

"Get real, Cassie. Nothing justifies him breaking your violin."

He's angry now, and I can't believe I've hurt the only person who's been nice to me since I ran away.

Whoosh! Jessica pulls the covers off me, leans down into my face, and gestures the sign for me to shut up.

I look up at her and whisper, "Sorry." Then I whisper to Nick, "I can't talk anymore."

"Call me tomorrow."

I pull the cover back over my head and make a cocoon where I can feel safe in this bedroom I'm sharing with a bunch of strangers. But my guilt over upsetting Nick is too large to fit in the small space. I pop my head back out and take deep breaths. I finally hear what he said before we hung up—he wants me to call him tomorrow. He can't be too mad if he still wants to talk to me.

Someone shakes me awake. It's Rachel. I quickly scoot away from her, bumping into a wall. "You'll miss breakfast," she says, walking toward the door.

My whole being fills with a sense of black as I remember I'm in a homeless shelter, until I realize that I can think about my violin goddess. That she'll keep me safe. I'll watch and listen for ways to be strong with each step I take today. Even though I don't know where I'm going next, just thinking about being strong gives me a sense of direction.

At breakfast, there's no real conversation among us, just little snippets of sound. It all sounds jittery; maybe it's just me, but maybe it's all of us, thinking about how big the world is outside of this shelter, and that we're about to go back out into it. I shovel Corn Flakes into my mouth. After the first helping, I fill my bowl again. I finish the second bowl, too.

"Anyone know of a pharmacy close by?" I ask.

"Yeah," says Jessica. "Come with us."

"We're planning to party the morning away in the

cosmetics section," says Rachel. "It'll give us something fun to do."

I look from Jessica to Rachel. She's acting like she didn't touch my boob last night. If Jessica's around, it should be safe. "Yeah, okay."

I notice lots of girls slipping fruit into their pockets, so I put a banana into the empty pocket of my hoodie.

Outside, it's crisp and sunny, and it almost distracts me from the stark trees. Rachel hooks her arm through Jessica's and I walk on the other side of her. We go about five blocks. Just when I'm beginning to feel too cold to keep walking, we reach the pharmacy. Inside, they head right to the makeup like they planned, while I wander around. In front of the magazine rack, I call Grandpa. Still no answer.

I scan the titles, looking for teen magazines. Instead, *Family Circle* catches my eye, with a long table set for a bunch of Thanksgiving guests on the cover. Little sound bytes advertise delicious recipes, Christmas crafts to make, and ways to deal with holiday stress. There's no article about how to deal with a dad who broke his daughter's violin just before Thanksgiving.

Then I wander around the store, stopping to look at the school supplies as if I'm searching for the perfect pen. Passing through the game section, I find the Magic Eight Ball toy still in its box. When I turn it over, a circular window is cut out so that I can see the blue triangle with the answer showing up in white letters. I turn the box around in my hands a few times. I decide to ask if I will ever play the violin again. It answers: "Rely on it." I ask if Calliope is okay. It answers: "Better not to tell you now." I shake it in the air.

Will I find the violin goddess? It says: "Can't tell." Then I tumble it in my hands a few times. Does Nick like me? It answers: "Without a doubt." I decide to stop on a positive note, replace the toy on the shelf, and wander off. In front of the automotive stuff, I call my grandfather again. Still no answer.

In cosmetics, Rachel's painting her left index finger-nail a deep shade of blue. "You like?" She practically pokes me in the eye with her finger.

"On you, yeah."

"But you wouldn't buy it?"

"I'm in the symphony. The conductor's picky about nails."

"You're in the symphony?"

"Yeah."

"What do you play? Wait. Let me guess. The flute?"

"No, the violin."

"Don't you have rehearsals like, every day?"

"Not anymore." I walk away. In front of the popcorn, I try Grandpa's number one more time, but he's still not an-swering. I wander over to the cashier, where an older woman wearing a baggy white sweater chats with a woman holding a baby. Her cheeriness makes me feel like I can ask her for directions, so I wander over to her register.

She smiles at me. "Can I help you?"

I dig out my grandfather's address. "Can you tell me how to get here?" I show her the piece of paper.

She adjusts her glasses, reads the address, then looks at me. "By bus?"

"No, I'm going to walk."

"It's a long walk."

"Could you give me directions?"

A woman gets in line behind me.

"Give me a minute." She waves the woman forward.

I step out of her way and wait until she and two more customers pay the cashier. Then the cashier grabs a pen and writes out the directions. Her handwriting is shaky. And between how slow she writes and the interruptions when she stops to take care of a couple more customers, I feel like I probably could've been halfway there by now.

"Thanks."

"Bundle up, hon."

I leave without saying goodbye to Rachel and Jessica. Out the door, I look all around, ready for a violin goddess sighting. The sun is out, but it's way too cold to be outside without a coat, scarf and gloves—which I am—so I walk as fast as I can.

As I speed along, I realize that the sooner I get there, the sooner I'll have to tell Grandpa about his violin. I consider not telling him. Then I decide: he should know what happened. I walk blocks and blocks, and it's enough mileage to rehearse five different ways to give him the bad news.

After a half hour I check the directions. I'm still only on the second out of five parts of the cashier's directions. My stomach churns and I reach into my pocket for the banana from the shelter. Then I put it back because I don't know when or how I'll get my next real meal. Up ahead I see a library, and as much as I want to get to Grandpa's before dark, I decide I need to make a pit stop.

Pushing my way through the door, I'm hit with a blast of heat. I rub my hands together as I try to locate the bathroom. After I find it and go, I run the hot water over my hands for a long time, imagining the warmth traveling deep into my bones, heating up my whole body. When a woman comes in, I step away from the sink to dry my hands on the wall dryer. I push the button for a second round of hot air, once again trying to absorb the heat, even though my hands are already dry.

I decide to pretend this is my library. I wander to the young adult section, reading book titles, then wander toward the magazines and a small area with chairs arranged in a circle. I grab *Elle Girl* magazine and fall back into an empty chair, one that doesn't face the window and the scene outside. I need a break from all that cold and want to forget about it for a while. Distracted, I flip through the pages, but none of the words are making sense. I close the magazine and lean my head back, telling myself not to shut my eyes. But I do.

Pizza and sugar fill the air at Venetian Fest. I'm on the octopus. Dad and me. The ride's starting up and that creep Harley jumps into the car with us. I try to get out, but it's moving faster now and it's too late to bolt. The car revs, moves from left to right and back again, rising. The air turns sour and burnt. Back and forth, the ride speeds up as Harley puts his arm around me. Lights flash all around us, as the ride jerks and yanks us from one end to the other, bounces us up high, and bumps me first into Dad, and then into Harley. The car is flying fast now and Dad falls out. I scream but no sound comes out of my mouth. Meanwhile, Harley holds me tighter. I can't smell anything. It's dark now. I can't see anything and I can't breathe. I start to scream, but Harley puts his hand over my mouth.

"Is this seat taken?"

The voice scares me and I jump, almost falling out of the chair.

"Sorry—I didn't mean to scare you," a girl about my age says, and then she walks away.

I sit there for another fifteen minutes, then force myself to get up to leave. As I approach the door, I can't face the rest of my long, cold trek, so from the warmth of the lobby, I call Grandpa one more time. It takes ten rings to sink in that I have to do more walking, like it or not.

It's hard, but I push myself to walk fast, to get into some kind of a rhythm. The wind picks up, and that's when, for the first time today, it occurs to me that I could do all this walking and Grandpa might not be home when I get there. Then, in an instant, I can't tell the difference between being cold and being afraid.

I call him again. No surprise. He's not there.

I slam my cell shut, then check the directions. I look up and see that I'm at the third step of the directions. I tell myself to keep going and then move into a slow jog. I should've thought of this sooner, because it's the warmest I've felt the whole time I've been outside. I jog through a small downtown area, and don't even care that the shoppers are looking at me like I'm some kind of wild animal. I jog until my side hurts, then settle back into walking.

When my stomach begins to growl, I eat the shelter banana in three bites without missing a beat in my stride.

I stop once more to check the directions. I'm almost there. And then it's like I shouldn't have stopped because I can hardly drag my feet to take the remaining steps to get where I'm trying to go. So I walk very slowly. Slow. Slow. Slow.

This must be my grandfather's house. I stand on the sidewalk under a gray sky and stare at a ranch house surrounded by a frozen, patchy lawn. Is this where Dad grew up? It's a new house so I doubt it, but it bugs me that I don't know for sure. Why don't I know anything about my grandfather? He's part of my family.

I ring the doorbell and wait. And wait some more. I turn halfway around and look across the street at the neighbor's house. The street is quiet. Then the sound of the door opening jolts me back. "Grandpa. Hi."

"Cassie?" He motions for me to come in, then points down the hallway.

Behind me, the sound of his slippers swooshing on the wood floor makes him seem really old and pathetic, and for a second I want to hug him hello. But when I stop and turn to look at him, he's close and it doesn't feel right. "Maybe I shouldn't have come." I start to get teary and look down at the floor.

"Nonsense," Grandpa says.

I wander into the living room. Grandpa shuffles a few steps behind me. I sit down on the couch and fold my hands on my lap.

My grandfather sits near me, on the edge of a recliner.

"Are you okay?" I ask.

"I just got back from the hospital." He shifts in the chair to get comfortable.

"You were in the hospital?"

"I came down with a fever when I got back from Chicago. Turns out, I was dehydrated. Needed IV fluids."

"Oh." *Do you tell a sick old person that their son broke the antique, really expensive violin he gave you?*

"Supposed to be record lows this month," Grandpa says. "You warm enough?"

I nod yes, even though I mean no. I didn't come here to discuss the weather.

"What brings you to Pretoria?"

"Well—" All of my muscles tense up.

"You okay?"

I start to say yes, and then I get teary. "Your violin—"

"Sounded magnificent at your concert." Grandpa taps the arm of the chair. "Glad I could make it."

It's hard to do this, even harder than I imagined, and it's difficult to continue. I put my face in my hands. All the energy it's taken to get here deserts me and I let myself cry. My sadness, frustration, and fatigue all come out in the form of tears. Then I take a breath, look at Grandpa, and between whimpers, I tell him. "He—Dad—he, uh, broke it." Through sobs, I say, "It's gone."

Grandpa withdraws and looks like Dad does when he's

angry. I imagine him trying not to blurt out a string of swear words, at the same time hoping his skin will hold firm against the explosion inside his mind.

"I'm sorry, Grandpa." I wipe my tears with the back of my hand.

"No need to apologize." He looks past me, out the window. "That's for Frank to do. It's about him, not you."

"No, it's about me. I should've fed the cat. Then she wouldn't have annoyed him."

He wrinkles his nose, looking confused.

I go into more detail and tell him exactly how it happened.

Grandpa shakes his head. "Frank never could control himself."

That can't be true. I lean toward him. "He's not always like that. Sometimes he's okay."

My grandfather's digging his hands into his thighs. A familiar alarm is going off inside my brain, and I feel like I should locate an emergency exit if he's going to blow like Dad does.

"When he was your age, Frank embarrassed me."

I squirm. I decide I really don't want to be here anymore.

"He couldn't handle the pressure."

"What are you talking about?" It comes out sounding like I don't believe him.

He starts to get out of the chair, stumbles back. "For christsakes!" My grandfather slowly heaves himself up and out of the chair, towers over me and yells right in my face, "Frank betrayed me." He points at the ground. "He betrayed the Prochazka name!"

"You're scaring me, Grandpa," I say, leaning as far away from him as I can get. "Don't yell, okay?"

"Shut the hell up!" he shouts.

I look at him, stunned. But he's staring across the room, like he's talking to the crystal bowl poised on top of the piano. "She never forgave me—she went to her grave blaming me—for Frank giving up the violin."

"Who never forgave you?"

"Your grandmother, Sophia." He's angry, but I can hear his guilt in the syllables of her name. "It's a long story. But after Frank and I fought, he flung his violin at the wall."

"What were you fighting about?"

"Never mind. Go on. Get out of here!" He shuffles out of the room.

"Grandpa, wait."

He doesn't stop.

I watch him go. His slippers slide along the wooden floor, away toward the other end of the house.

In a daze, I stand up. I wander in the direction where Grandpa went. I find him in a small family room, watching TV with his back to me.

"Grandpa?" I walk a little closer, thinking maybe he didn't hear me. Then, standing at his side, I say, "Grandpa?"

He sits there, stares straight ahead at Vanna turning those damn letters, as if I don't exist.

"Well, okay. I'm going now."

I turn around to leave and get teary. I wander into the kitchen, not ready yet to face the cold again—I had expected to stay here tonight. All that's in the fridge is a half dozen eggs, a quart of milk, and a pack of American cheese. I snatch two slices of cheese. Jackets hang on a coat tree by the door. I grab a brown one, put it on, and zip up. The sleeves are too long and the jacket hangs almost to my knees, but who cares? On my way out, I notice a dish holding a few dollars and some change. I dump all of it into the coat pocket.

Outside, I start walking and don't know where I'm going. I eat both cheese slices. Then, after a few blocks, the question hits me like a snowball on my head: What is up with this family and the violin? Dad intensely hates it. He's already destroyed two. And Grandpa—he's still obsessed and furious about a fight he had with Dad that probably happened more than twenty years ago, about a different violin. I hate to admit it, but if Grandpa was this mean to Dad when he was my age, then I'm starting to feel sorry for Dad.

As I retrace my steps, the neighborhood is more alive now. I walk another block, when a car pulls into a driveway at the next house. A woman about my mom's age gets out of the car. I approach her slowly, and ask her for directions to the nearest fast-food place.

"Which one?" she asks.

"Any one. Or a grocery store. Any kind of food store will do."

"Are you a runaway? I read about teen runaways just the other day."

"No, I'm meeting someone, and he can't come for a while so I want to wait somewhere warm."

"How can you meet someone if you don't know where you're going?"

The wind is rattling her grocery bags, my bones are already cold, and now she wants to know my life story. I really want to strangle her. "Uh, ma'am, please. Can you give me some directions?"

She points to the right and gives me an elaborate set of directions to a Subway sandwich shop. I repeat them back to her, to make sure I got what she said. "Oh, and there's a cute store for kids. Oh, well, forget it. It's for little kids."

Inside Subway, I check my messages to see if Winnie

found Calliope. "Cass, hey, it's Tuesday, where are you? I just talked to your mom. Calliope's back there. I'm so sorry. Call me."

"Ohmygod!"

"Can I help you, miss?"

You can beam me home to pick up my cat. The smell of bread baking makes me want to ask for a foot-long sub sandwich. But since I'm broke, I order a cup of chicken noodle soup instead. She ladles it out of the pot while I listen to the message Mom left about fifteen minutes ago. "Cassie, I cannot believe you are all the way in Pretoria! Call me. I'm on my way to pick you up."

My heart speeds up at the thought of Mom driving down here. I'm still in shock over my broken violin, and stunned at what just happened at Grandpa's. And now I hear that Calliope's back home. No way—I'm not going home—except I have to protect my cat.

I pay for my soup, and on my way over to a table by the window, I notice the clock on the wall. It's 3:45. The soup warms me from the inside out, reaching my face and hands. Except it doesn't thaw my heart. My anger at my grandfather freezes on top of my ice-cold rage at Dad.

I punch in Winnie's number. When she answers, I start in midsentence, telling her what's going on.

"Cass! I can't stay on. My lesson's starting. I know your mom gets on your nerves, but I'm glad you're coming home."

"I never said that. I said 'Jeannine's coming to Pretoria.' I don't want to come home."

"Then have your mom drop you off at my house.

Sorry, but I have to go." She hangs up without saying good-bye, and I know this means she's walking with her cello into Mrs. Harris's studio. I envy her, getting to take a lesson.

I'm just about going crazy from too many thoughts pulsating in my brain at once. That's when I decide that moving in the cold would actually be better than sitting still here. So I go back outside. I put my hands in the big coat pockets and walk down the street. At first, I'm walking fast, with a quick, clipped rhythm. My ears are already cold, and I wish I'd thought to steal a hat from Grandpa, too. When I slow down, I start to notice the neighborhood. The houses are smaller here than they were where Grandpa lived. Some of the storefronts are boarded up. No one is out walking. Now and then cars go by, all turning into the gas station at the corner. After they gas up they pull out and keep going, heading away from me. I panic, thinking about the sun going down soon. I don't want to be out here in this unfamiliar neighborhood when it's dark.

A lady bundled up like a mummy passes me, walking her dog. I turn around and watch her go, thinking I maybe should follow her so I'm not out here alone. But I don't want to go back the way I just came because there's nothing back there.

I get this overwhelming urge to play my violin. Since I can't, I deal with it the same way I deal with math class. I imagine sheet music on a stand in front of me and walk through the notes in my brain. This time, I pick *Candide*. And since I'm not in math class, I begin to hum out loud. I hum and breathe, singing the notes the way they would sound coming from my violin. I go on like this for blocks. And in my mind, I even can hear Winnie on the cello; and there's the bassoon and the tympani. For blocks and blocks I'm lost in a private concert, playing alongside an imaginary violin goddess.

The color purple stops me—stops my humming. It's barely light out anymore, but the small church is glowing, its purple stained-glass windows reflecting the setting sun. The church's light calls to me and I walk the short path toward the front door. Halfway up the path I read the sign out front: Epiphany Church. By the door I see that the siding is painted a deep lilac. It looks to me like a house where a goddess would live. Maybe mine's inside. I pull the handle, am relieved that it's not locked, and walk inside.

It's dark except for the small altar off to the right; it's filled with rows and rows of tiny white votive candles, each in a glass holder. A short woman is standing there, with the hood of her parka still up. I walk toward her as she drops a coin in a collection box. When I get there, she says, "It's not much, but a penny *is* a donation."

I agree, and dig one of Grandpa's pennies out of my pocket. I drop it into the box, too.

She strikes a match and when it whispers, she transfers the flame from matchstick to candlewick. One by one, she lights each candle like she's working a conveyor belt. "My friend has cancer—I'm lighting them for her—she's back at the house in so much pain." She goes to the front of the church, kneels, pushes off her hood, smoothes down her hair, and then puts her hands together in prayer.

I strike a match. The flame is big, and when I look at it, it warms my cheeks. I touch the flame to the wick, and the candle whooshes into light. I don't feel scared anymore. After a few seconds, I light another candle and keep going, lighting an entire row. Before long, I can't tell if the light is inside of me or outside.

After a while, I head for a seat near the back, in a pew close to the candle altar, where I can be near the glow and the warmth. The cold bench creaks when I sit down, and I raise my head to look up at the rafters. The old church is drafty, and I cross my arms and legs to keep warm. I take deep breaths, and this breathing makes me think of Miss Sinclair. I hope she'll forgive me for missing my violin lesson yesterday. I get teary then, lean over, put my face in my hands, and start to cry. With the tears come images that float in my brain. My shattered violin. Dad's sick smile when he threw it. Calliope scurrying off outside. Musical notes not attached to a page, flying, getting mixed up, and hurting my ears. Tears come faster, and sobs make my whole body shake.

"Hey, hey."

Her voice is close, but her hand on my back startles me. I jump.

"Hon—shh, shh, it's gonna be okay." She puts her arm around me, but I don't lean into her like I want to.

"I'm so lost and I'm trying to find my way."

"Prayers said here definitely get answered, eventually. Maybe it's not exactly like we plan, but there's always direction, an answer."

I don't see a way out of this mess.

"Is there someone you can call?"

I look up at her.

"You seem like a girl who would be cared about by a lot of people."

Her kindness reaches me. "My violin teacher."

"Do you have a cell phone?"

I nod my head.

She hands me a crumpled-up tissue. "Call her." She points to the foyer in the back of the church. "You'll get a good signal back there."

I wipe my tears as I get up to call Miss Sinclair.

She answers on the first ring. "Cassie! Where are you? Your mom's worried sick."

"I'm sorry about missing my lesson yesterday."

"Winnie called. Don't worry about it. Honey, tell me—where are you?"

I can't answer because the tears are blocking my words.

"Cassie, listen to me, okay?" She pauses. "It's going to be okay. I'll help you. But first you have to let me come get you."

"I can't go home."

"You have to stop . . . stop running away from things."

"He broke my violin—*my own dad*. I can't deal with it."

"The Cassie I know can handle this. All of it."

"You're wrong."

"I've known you for a long time. You have to let go of your fear. Make space for the strength inside you to take over."

"Miss Sinclair, do you believe in goddesses?"

"I do."

"You do? Really?"

"In fact there's probably one watching out for you right now."

I look toward the altar. The woman has resumed kneeling.

"I'm in Pretoria. Mom's on her way."

"You've talked to her then."

"No, I got a message."

"When will she be there?"

"I don't know. I'm scared."

"I hear that, but your mom—she's a different person. This situation—it's made her see things she was blind to before. You have to give her a chance."

"You think it's okay? I mean, to go home?"

"I do."

"He has to stop breaking things."

"Cassie, I'm so sorry. I didn't know all this was going on."

"He smashed Mom's favorite vase, he broke his computer, smashed the wall, and now my violin."

"That tells me how strong you are . . . you learned your solo while you were living with all that violence."

"I can't live with it anymore."

"Your mom's committed to changing that."

"But what about Dad? He'll only love me if I quit the violin."

"It doesn't have to be that way."

"I think it does."

"Call your mom. Talk it out with her. Promise me you will."

"Okay." I sniff. "Thank you."

Before I lose my courage, I call Jeannine.

"Cassie." She pauses. I can hear her trying not to cry. "Sweetheart, please, I love you. Come home."

"Is Calliope okay?"

"She's fine."

"Where's Dad?"

"He's . . . not here. He's not with me. Please, let's talk

about this in person. I need you to tell me exactly where you are."

"Hold on. I'll get the address." I walk outside and peer at the sign. A tiny spotlight shows the address, just below the schedule for Sunday services. I read it to her.

"I'll set my GPS and be there right away."

I take deep breaths . . . inhale . . . and exhale slowly. *Hold on, Calliope. I'll be home soon.*

23

Once at a lesson, when I was first learning my solo, my A string was out of tune and I kept lifting my bow off the string too much. I just couldn't get the timing, but Miss Sinclair told me she believed I could play it. She said she'd go on believing until I knew it myself. Right now, shivering in this church foyer, waiting to face Jeannine, I hope Miss Sinclair's believing in me again. I hope that this is the right step to be taking—going back home. Because every part of me is shaking, telling me I shouldn't do it. I'm only going home to protect Calliope, not because I want to stop running.

When Jeannine pulls up, I look back at the woman who is still praying. I whisper, "Thank you."

"Godspeed," she says out loud.

I open the door and walk down the short path to Jeannine's gold Mercedes. It looks very out of place in this run-down neighborhood. She jumps out of the car and I'm shocked to see her wearing her black leather jacket over a pair of old gray sweats. Usually if she's going out in public, she's very picky about how she looks. Now she's all over me, hugging me and pulling me close. But I don't hug her back. She holds on too long, smothering me with her overpowering perfume and I finally have to shift out of her hug so I can breathe. I mean, I'm glad to finally feel safe again, but right now, I'm hearing what my heart has been whispering for months: I'm mad at her—burning mad.

"Are you okay?" She opens her car door.

"Fine. I'm fine." I get in beside her.

"I'm so glad to see you, Cassie."

Facing straight ahead, I stare out the front windshield. I buckle my seat belt as little flakes of snow are fluttering all around.

"Are you hungry?" She puts the key in the ignition, then adjusts the mirror.

"Let's just go home, okay?"

"There's a hotel close to here, near the highway."

"I need to see Calliope."

"I'm too tired to drive back tonight. I sent her home with Debra."

"Your assistant?"

"Yes. I've been leaning on her since you left." She punches at the GPS screen on the dashboard. "I have to concentrate now. We can talk when we get to the hotel."

"Fine." I lean my head back and close my eyes. I can't believe she told anyone about our problems. She's always so worried about what people think. But I'm glad she told Debra. Debra's cool. I picture her carrying Calliope out of our house in a pet carrier, and I call out to my baby girl. *Don't worry, Calliope. You're not going to the vet.* She hates going to the vet. *You're going someplace nice. Take a lot of naps and I'll see you soon.* The heat blasting out of the vents feels cozy and I start to relax, appreciating Jeannine's luxurious, heated leather seats like never before.

"There's a diner next to the hotel." She pulls out of the parking space and onto the deserted street.

"Sure." I look over at Jeannine. Her hair is all wild around her head. I can't remember ever seeing her like this. Even on the weekends, she showers as soon as she's out of bed, then styles her hair into a perfect poufy golden cut. I'm shocked that she's out looking like this, and even wants to go to a restaurant not looking perfect.

Inside the diner there're only a few other customers. A waitress tells us to sit wherever we want, and Jeannine chooses a booth near the back wall, off in the corner. I slide in, feeling excited to be getting an audience with her, but I'm also totally mad at her for checking out of our family all this time. For ages we haven't talked about anything other than schedules, and I can't remember when we actually had dinner together. I hide behind the big menu to buy myself some time to figure out which way to play it and what I'm going to say.

Jeannine doesn't order her usual chicken Caesar salad; instead she gets meatloaf, mashed potatoes, and a side of green bean casserole. I order macaroni and cheese. We pass our menus to the waitress and she walks away. Jeannine says, "Comfort food."

Maybe so. "I just ordered it because it sounds good."

Jeannine clasps her hands, rests them on the table, then looks at me. I flash back to "Take Your Daughter to Work Day," when she opened the pitch meeting for a new ad campaign. If her hair wasn't so wild and out of control, I'd think she was going into meeting mode right now. Except there's something different shining in her eyes—a sadness that she's been afraid to show before this.

"Well," she said. "We should probably get you to the doctor tomorrow."

"Why? I'm not sick."

"To make sure you're okay."

"Mom, I left because Dad's the one who's crazy."

"Shh, honey." She lowers her chin and whispers at me, "Please, lower your voice."

"Then let's not talk about Dad in public."

"Fair enough."

The waitress brings Jeannine a side salad and sets between us a round basket filled with dinner rolls. I take out a piece of crusty bread. It reminds me of the red plastic basket at the shelter—only that one was filled just with white bread, not the rye and muffins and sourdough this one holds. I immediately feel glad not to be worrying about my next meal anymore.

"How's Calliope?"

"She has a scratch on her face—"

"A scratch?"

Jeannine traces a line just above her right eye to show me. "She must've gotten into a fight in the alley."

I put my hand up to my mouth. Thinking of her in danger makes me almost cry.

"It's healing. She's fine. Really."

I set the bread down and look away, thinking how much I need Calliope to be okay.

When our food comes we eat in silence. I have a lot of questions I want to ask her. *Why didn't you do anything when Dad hurled your favorite vase at the wall? What did you do with the Mangenot? Did you throw it out? Is it in the trash or in the recycling bin? Want to place bets on what he'll destroy next?* But I don't ask any of them because we'll just get into a fight, and neither of us wants to do that here.

We end up checking into a motel kind of hotel. Jeannine surprises me again when she wants to stay here. Usually when we go on vacation, she makes reservations in a luxury high-rise place, complete with a concierge. She opens the trunk of the car and lifts out a big black trash bag. "There wasn't time to pack," she says, when she sees me staring dumbstruck at the bag. "I had Debra throw some things together for us."

When she goes to shut the trunk, I see my violin case. I put my hand over my heart in shock. It looks like a little coffin now. "Why'd you bring that?"

"Don't you carry something for good luck?"

She must be referring to the navy velveteen pouch with the pink quartz turtle that I carry in the violin case. But it's not for good luck. A gift from Miss Sinclair—she'd given it to me when I made first chair in the youth symphony. It's for love and patience. Which is what I definitely need right now. I grab the case and the lightness of it throws me off balance.

I get distracted from the heavy feeling in my chest when I see our room. It's really cold, like the heater here has never, ever worked. I walk all the way into the room, turn

on a light, and see that I'm walking on old green shag car-
pet. Jeannine turns a few knobs on the heat register below
the window. Air blows out and lifts the pink flowered curtains. When I set my case on the bed, it's right beside a cigarette burn on the rust-colored coverlet.

"Interesting decorating scheme," Jeannine says. "At
least it looks clean." She sets down the trash bag and heads
past me into the bathroom.

While she's in there, I sit down beside my violin case
and unlatch the lid. I slowly lift it and smell the familiar
scent of Orchestra Hall—wood and varnish, and tarnished
brass—and this makes it difficult to face the empty space
where my violin used to be. My rosin's there, and the small
purple journal where I keep notes on what to practice. I take
out the little pouch and slip out the rose quartz turtle. It's
cool in my hand, and I rub my thumb over the scales on the
turtle's back, remembering Miss Sinclair saying, "Love and
patience are the recipe for good music." When Jeannine
emerges from the bathroom, I close the case with one hand,
sheltering the turtle in the other.

"Okay, who's showering first?" She claps her hands
together.

It amazes me, that with all that's happened, she can
still come up with her "manager" voice, directing us, pushing us to be productive. I don't reply.

She tilts her head. "What is it?"

"I just thought, you know, that we'd talk first." I point
at her bed.

"And I think we'll be able to tolerate each other better
if we smell good." She turns to go back into the washroom.

"Don't you care about what happened to me?"

That stops her. She turns to face me. "Of course I do. So much so that I never even got a shower today."

I clench the turtle in my hand.

"Forgive me for trying to make you comfortable."

"Sounds like nothing's changed!" I pound the bed.

"What's that supposed to mean?"

"My violin's broken and all you care about is how you look." I point at her.

She sits down beside me. "Okay, Cassie." She lets out a sigh. "I wanted to wait until we'd cleaned up, but I guess we'll talk right now. I'm sorry to have to tell you this, but I told your dad to move out. He left on Sunday night."

Shocked, I begin rocking. Rocking, andante rocking.

"I had to. To protect you."

I stop rocking. "Great. So now I'm a home wrecker."

"No, don't—what is it you kids say—don't go there! If anyone's the home wrecker, it's him."

"I should've fed Calliope right away." I flop backward, to lie on the bed. "Then this wouldn't be happening."

"That's ridiculous. I should have told him last summer that breaking my vase was unacceptable. I should have dealt with that outburst right away."

This gets my attention. I sit back up. In all my life, I've never heard Jeannine admit a mistake.

"I knew your father wasn't happy about you becoming a violinist. I mean—he didn't approve of me buying your first violin—but then he stayed out of it. So I certainly never imagined he'd destroy it." And then she crumples. Puts her face in her hands and cries.

This is so unlike Jeannine, to cry. To let me see her being anything but cheerful. I put my hand on her back.

"I'm so sorry." She stands to get a tissue from the washroom. "The only way I could deal with him was to hide out by burying myself in my work. I see that now. And it wasn't fair to you." She sits back down, lets out a breath, and then cries harder, dabbing at her eyes with a tissue.

I begin to rub her back.

She looks into my eyes. "When I saw you leave, when I saw you run out of our house like you were rescuing Calliope from a fire, I knew right then that this finally had to stop."

I cross my arms over my chest. "I can't live with the violence any longer."

"Neither can I." She nods her head.

"What are we going to do?" Now I start to cry.

She puts her arm around me and I lean into her shoulder. There are so many things about her that drive me nuts. The way she forgets about me until it's concert time, then pretends I'm the center of the universe, turning me into her human Barbie doll, taking me shopping at her favorite boutique to find the perfect dress. The way she just stopped coming home for dinner, leaving me stuck fixing meals for Dad, who hasn't been in a good mood since, like, forever. But I need a mom—I need her to be *my* mom, so I let her hold me until there're no more tears left.

The hot water isn't steady, so we end up taking super quick showers. When I get out, I wrap myself in a towel and ask Mom if she brought me any pajamas. On my bed I see a purple rainbow of my clothes. I smile, remembering when Debra and I had the conversation about being purple people. I'm into other colors these days, but it was sweet of her to pack my favorite violet flannel pajamas with lavender butterflies. They're faded, but what I really appreciate is their scent, so clean and familiar.

"Winnie called." Mom says, already in bed. "You didn't answer your cell so she called me. So did Eva Sinclair. They both wanted to make sure you're coming home. And your brother says hello."

"He called?" It's only 9:30, but I'm exhausted so I turn out the light and get under the covers in the other bed.

"I called him. To let him know you're safe. He's coming home this weekend."

"Mom, where *is* Dad?" The room is so quiet. Like it and the entire universe outside of it is listening for her answer.

"For now, he's living at a hotel. In town. The one near Eva's studio."

"Are we ever going to be a family again?"

"Honey, I don't know. I hope so, but I really don't know. It all depends."

"On what?"

"On your dad."

"You mean if he gets a personality makeover?"

"Don't say that. It's mean."

"He's mean."

"I hope to get back the nice man I married."

"And this will happen how?"

"By making him leave, it forces him to get help. That's what the therapist suggested."

"You saw a therapist?"

"Debra recommended her."

"I'm surprised you went."

"I don't know how I got so sidetracked. This family has to come first, and I see that now."

It's going to take time, to get used to this new person—this Jeannine who is my mother.

"Cassie, I'm fading. Let's talk in the morning." She turns over with her back to me.

I'm so tired, but I can't sleep. I turn over, too, with my back to Mom, and face the wall.

Donna, our Girl Scout leader, drops me off after the meeting. I run-skip-run, happy, up the stairs. I can't wait for our camping trip this weekend! Hiking all day. And s'mores and ghost stories around the campfire.

Inside is a symphony. I follow the music to the living room, which is filled with Beethoven's Violin Concerto. I stop when I see Dad, facing the window and bowing in time to the music. He's playing an invisible violin. He's graceful, not fidgety like when he's working on the computer. I stand there, keeping my presence a secret, so I can watch Dad being something I've never seen before: a light and easy dancer, acting out a body language not new to me, but one that I didn't know he understood. Each note comes out strong, pure, and vibrant.

I tiptoe up the stairs, then, just as quietly, come back down.

"Here." I hand my violin to him.

He jerks around. It isn't the Artist, which I outgrew. It's my three-quarter-size violin, my Hermione. Dad looks at it, making me think he's going to take it and run his hand over the thick maple varnish. But instead, he looks at the floor for a few seconds. Then, when he remembers I'm still there, he looks at me. "No." He blinks, and for a moment I wonder if he's going to cry. Then he says, "Uh, no. That's okay."

I hide the violin behind my back as Dad fumbles over the buttons on the CD player, finally punching it off. Dead air replaces the music.

The sound of my mom turning over jars me. It takes me a few seconds to remember where I am; and the quiet in the strange room makes me remember that day, when Dad shut off the music. I was so sad then. And I still keep wondering why he gave up the violin when he'd looked so happy, pretending to play.

Like the old mom, this new mom is a morning person. She gets me up at seven and we head for home. She's businesslike again. In the daylight, I can see that her car is immaculate, and everything's in its place in the organizer between the seats—tissues, coins for the meters, her key card for the downtown garage. I know she's on a mission when she tells me we're not stopping for breakfast, but that instead we're doing drive-thru. She's actually okay about me eating in her car!

We get our orders and I'm careful not to get crumbs all over the place. When I'm done eating and we're settled into a smooth driving speed, I move to turn on the radio.

"No, please." She glances at me. "Don't turn it on."

She's never minded music before.

"I want to talk to you."

Her tone makes me wonder if there's more bad news.

She grasps the steering wheel white-knuckle tight. "This is hard, but I really need to know some things."

"Like what?" Outside the windshield, the morning is cloudy and gray.

"Things. Such as how did you get to Pretoria?"

"By bus."

"You had enough money for the fare?" She leans closer to the windshield to check the exit sign.

"I used my lunch money and allowance."

"Where'd you sleep Sunday night?" She veers off, taking the exit for home.

"On the bus."

"Oh."

"Is that it?" I ask.

"No." She taps the steering wheel. "Where'd you sleep Monday night?"

I shift in my seat to face her. "Mom, why are we talking about this?"

"Because I need to know everything that happened to you." She points at me.

"Nothing happened."

"Did anyone touch you, you know, inappropriately?"

I don't want to talk about Rachel so I say no and nothing more.

"So where *did* you sleep on Monday night?"

"At a homeless shelter."

She lets out a sigh. Gripping the steering wheel, she pulls herself to sit up straight.

"It was for teens, Mom. It was okay." I shift around, facing forward again. The sky is so cloudy, like it's never going to be blue ever again.

"How'd you get to your grandfather's?"

"I walked."

Then it hits me. If she wants to play twenty questions, then I have some for her, too.

107

"I want to ask *you* something, Mom. Why'd you invite him to my concert, anyway? He's a total jerk."

"I'm astonished that he didn't show better judgment, letting you—his own granddaughter—walk the streets instead of having you stay with him. At least he finally had enough sense to call me."

"Did you know Dad broke his own violin?"

"No, I didn't." She glances at her side mirror. "But that *can't* be."

"Why would Grandpa make it up? I bet you don't even know that Dad smashed his computer last week."

"He did *what*?"

"You were still at work. I was scared so I had Winnie's sister come get me and Calliope. That's why I was over at her house so late on a school night. I didn't want to come back until you were home."

She touches my shoulder. "Cassie, why didn't you tell me?"

"I was too upset and afraid to say anything."

She strokes my shoulder until my cell phone rings.

Nick asks, "Where are you?"

"With my mom. I'm going home."

"Are you okay?"

"I guess so."

"You can't talk, can you?"

"Not really."

"I'll call you later."

"Good—please do. I'd really like to talk again."

I hang up, look at Mom, and say, "It's my turn again."

"Your turn?"

"To ask you another question. Why are Dad and Grandpa so mad at each other?"

"I don't really know, but they've been on the outs for years. I was hoping your concert might put an end to that."

I switch on the radio. This time she doesn't stop me. The songs distract me from thinking about how much I don't want to go home. The closer we get, the edgier I feel. When I look over at Mom she seems focused on driving, but I wonder what she's thinking.

As we wait at the light on the exit ramp, a homeless man approaches on Mom's side of the car. He's holding a paper cup up to the window. Mom pretends she doesn't see him.

"Roll down the window!" I say.

"No, Cass. It's not safe."

"Give him this." I hand over an apple from the shelter.

She stares at it like I'd just handed her a rat.

"Mom, please."

She finally takes it, holds it with two fingers, and dangles her arm out the window.

"Thanks, ma'am" is all he says.

But Mom doesn't look at him. As the light changes, she steps on the gas while she's closing her window.

After she turns, I ask, "Is my broken violin still in the sink?"

"No, Cassie. I wrapped it up in one of your old baby blankets, put it in a box, and sealed it. It's on a shelf in my closet. I couldn't bear to throw it out."

For some reason, this makes me feel a little better.

A pack of butterflies trembles near my heart when we get to our street. I'm horrified to see Dad's Jeep parked in front of our house. He gets out and walks behind us as Mom pulls into the driveway. "What's he doing here?" I lock my door in a panic.

Mom doesn't answer.

"I'm not getting out of this car until he leaves."

She opens her door and gets out, closing it behind her. I instantly hit the lock button again. She leans against the car on her side. Dad's at mine, his fists balled up inside his gloves. I brace myself, half expecting him to pound on the roof above my head. After saying hello, they walk toward the house to talk. I can't tell what they're saying, but Mom doesn't look too upset.

Then he walks back toward the car, leans down, and looks in my window. "Can I talk to you?"

I shake my head no.

"Okay, okay. Just listen for a second, then." He crouches down and holds on to the car to steady himself. "I'm sorry, Cassie." He looks into my eyes like he's making sure the words got through the window. He keeps looking at me, reading me for a response.

I turn away and stare at the bay window of our house. There's a light on. A small part of me *is* glad he apologized. But an even bigger part is still too numb to hear it.

Then he gets back in his Jeep and slowly drives away. I unlock Mom's door. "What did he want?"

She reaches for her purse. "He wanted to know if you're okay."

"Like he cares." I push open my door.

"Of course he cares."

"Then why'd he break my violin?"

"He hopes you'll be able to forgive him." She shuts her door.

I slam my door and walk toward the house, checking the street in case he decided to come back.

I exhale as Mom unlocks the front door. Inside I smell a hint of the familiar air freshener and I stand there, stuck. Sadness fills me up: my violin is gone—this is all real. Dad really did destroy my violin—it's not just a bad dream. It's really gone forever.

Calliope doesn't come to meet me. The house feels so empty without her.

"I'm going to my room." I drag myself up the stairs like someone is pulling me up after them. I shut my door, flop down on the bedspread, and stare up at my Joshua Bell poster. I half expect Calliope to jump up on the bed.

As I lie there, I wonder: *What am I supposed to do with Dad's apology? Forgive and forget? Act like nothing happened? No way!*

Unable to settle down, I go back downstairs to talk to Mom about picking up Calliope. She's sitting at the kitchen table, talking on the phone and laughing. She sounds like someone I don't know—almost like Winnie and me when we're laughing at nothing. When she sees me she says, "I need to get going, Debra."

"You're acting like everything's fine." I shout at her from the doorway.

"I'm relieved," she says, coming over to stand beside me. "You're home safe and it feels great to relax a little." She exhales.

"Did you ask her about Calliope?"

"Yes. She's doing great." Mom sets her coffee mug down in the sink. "Debra's kids played with her all day yesterday."

"Can we pick her up tonight?"

"Tomorrow." She turns to look at me.

"Why not tonight? I really miss her!"

"It's not going to work out. Debra's not going to be home until late."

This news makes me feel like I'm going to lose it. But then I notice that the window above the sink—where the violin crashed—has been fixed. The smooth clarity of the glass makes me sigh. To me it's like a new marker on a grave.

I never thought I'd miss going to school, but after not being there these last three days, I actually do. Since we got back late in the morning, I stayed home today, and the day was long and boring without seeing my friends, without playing the violin. It's especially lonely without Calliope. At 3:05 p.m., I call Winnie on her cell. She's already worked it out that her sister'll drop her off here.

When she shows up she goes all mushy on me, wanting to hug me like she hasn't seen me in a year. She asks me repeatedly if I'm okay. Once we're in my room, I sit on the pillow that's leaning against the headboard. She sits facing me on the end of the bed and looks around. There's so much to say, but neither of us says a word. She finally breaks the silence, asking, "Why's Calliope's litter box in here?"

I had forgotten all about it. After Dad had one of his episodes, around the time Michael left for school, I moved the box up here from the basement. Now it's like another piece of furniture that I hardly notice. "Whenever Dad's home, I keep her in here. He hates her."

"Really?"

"I needed to keep her here, out of his way—so she'd be safe. But I forgot that day and left my door open."

"Where is she? I thought she'd be Velcroed to you."

"She's at Mom's assistant's house."

Winnie looks confused so I explain. Then she says, "It's not like you've been gone a long time, but we have a lot to catch up on."

"That's for sure, Win. It's rough out there. On the streets, I mean." I shift to sit cross-legged, same as Winnie. "I feel sorry for the homeless."

"Cass, I told you my dad would've picked you up. You didn't need to go through all that."

"Win, you have no idea what I've been through, so just shut up." I slap my thighs.

"I'm sorry, Cass"—she scoots closer and touches my knee—"I just meant that my parents wouldn't have minded if you stayed with us. That's all."

I pull my knees in close and wrap my arms around them. Winnie's my best friend, but right now, I'm so jealous of her. Her cello's intact. Her parents are cool. She's been in school all week and doesn't have to do a ton of makeup work. It makes me want to scream at her.

"What are you going to do about your violin?" she asks.

"What can I do?" I rest my head on my knees, avoiding the intensity of her question.

"You should call Anal Al."

"And get yelled at?" I mumble into my knee.

"I don't know, Cass. Maybe he can help. And anyway, how can you *not* tell the conductor about your violin?"

I was looking forward to seeing Winnie, but now that she's here, she's kind of making things worse and I'm getting edgy. "I want to talk to Miss Sinclair first."

"That's a great idea. Let's go over there."

"Now?"

"Why not? Call her."

"Most people would worry about school first and CYSO second." She looks at me in the mirror, where she's now standing, nervously playing with her hair. "But you're our soloist, so it has to be the other way around." She turns around then, clasps her hands, and says, "C'mon, Cass. You know I'm here for you no matter what."

She's hard to hate. I smile at her, grab my cell, and punch in Miss Sinclair's number. "She said to come at five."

Winnie says, "Give me some paper."

I dig out a notebook from my backpack, and Winnie starts a "to do" list, complete with categories for violin and school, hyperorganized, just like my mom.

After my runaway incident, Mom's nervous about me going out. But she did agree that visiting Miss Sinclair was a good idea and ends up giving me a ride. In front of the music studio she reminds me to call when I'm ready to come home.

I nod and get out of the car. I can see her watching me in the rearview mirror as she drives away to take Winnie home.

When she's out of sight, I'm radar girl, looking all around since Dad's hotel is right around the corner. I'm still not ready to see him. And I'm not ready to talk to him, either. And I'm definitely not ready to forgive him. Maybe I never will be.

Miss Sinclair opens her door before I even have a chance to ring the bell. "Cassie, come in." She puts her arm around me and walks me from the foyer into her studio. "After the performance you gave Saturday night, I was prepared to wear sunglasses, thinking you'd still be sparkling."

I try to smile, but I feel awkward and look away. I wish I was a big sunbeam instead of a girl with a broken violin.

"Sit down." She pats the piano bench beside her.

I sit down and look around the room at Miss Sinclair's mementos from all her tours: the framed print from her concert in Umbria, her lacquered music box from Berlin, and the black Nippon vase from Japan on the shelf with her music books. Their familiarity comforts me.

"I don't want to quit the youth symphony," I say.

She puts her arm around me, pulls me close, and clutches me firmly. "He can break all the violins in the world, but he *cannot* destroy your musical soul." I look up at her and her brown eyes are so close, it's like I can see her watching my brain work to decode her words.

"But if I keep playing, maybe I won't even have a family."

"That's fear talking. You have to let go of it." She swats at the air.

I sit on my hands. "But it's really hard."

"Love and patience aren't only a recipe for making good music, you know. They also apply to family."

For a few seconds I stare at the Umbria print by the window, following the red and orange strokes that make up the flowers growing on the hillside.

"You know, a goddess might view this as an opportunity, Cassie. A real chance to grow."

"It's hard to see how a demolished violin, separated parents, and an abused cat add up to a growth opportunity."

"I know, I know." She pats my leg. "But a divine, goddesslike way to look at it is to see that these things are happening for a reason, exactly like they're supposed to." She raises her hands up toward the ceiling. "And at the right time."

"No offense, Miss Sinclair, but that sounds kind of psycho."

She smiles. "Seriously, Cassie, I want you to try to accept what has happened."

"Forgive and forget?"

"Forgive? Maybe. Forget?" She shakes her head back and forth. "No. You probably won't ever forget."

I turn toward her and plead: "Would you call my conductor for me?"

"Already done."

"He yelled, right?"

"No. Quite the opposite." She pulls a file from the shelf beside her. "We're working on finding a benefactor to lend you a violin." She shows me an application filled out in her loopy handwriting.

I feel something bounce from my stomach into my heart, like hope with springs.

"It's not perfect, I know. It won't be like having your own violin. . . ."

She closes the file and I look at her, wishing I could have my own violin back, magically repaired. But then, that's not acceptance, is it?

". . . but," she goes on, crossing her fingers, "if it works out, you'll get to play a very special violin." Her little smile brings out her left dimple and hints at a bit of a wild streak.

"So I'm forwarding this application to Allen and he's contacting the Stradivari Society. We'll see what we can do." Then she gets quiet, like she's trying to figure out how to tell me the next part. I want to tell her to spit it out already.

Finally, she says, "Allen told me that if you don't have a violin by the new year, he'll be forced to look for a new soloist."

I grip the ridges of the bench and don't say what I'm thinking: *Over my dead body!*

Miss Sinclair checks her watch. "We've still got a little time to do some work today," she says, standing.

"How?"

"You can use my violin." She goes to the other side of the room, gets her violin out of the closet, and hands it to me.

Standing, I take her violin and face the mirror we use to check our posture and technique. I tune the instrument, then start with scales; I'm not smooth. It's hard knowing I've already lost something in only a few days without practicing. But I keep playing. I start out thinking I'm going to try my solo, but instead I end up playing "Amazing Grace."

On the piano bench, Miss Sinclair closes her eyes. She folds her hands, palms together, her fingers making a pointed steeple.

Was blind, but now, I see. . . . I go slow and try to get my position right, to find my way back in. Playing, pleading, calling out to the goddess, hoping she answers. Then I finish playing.

In the silence Miss Sinclair opens her eyes. "You must always find a way to make music."

I hand the violin back to her. I'm shaken, but in a good way.

"I'm sending you home with one of my old violins." She opens her closet door and hands me a battered black case. "Now go take good care of yourself. And practice!"

I clutch the tattered handle. "Thanks, Miss Sinclair. You're the best."

"A bubble bath is in order," she says, patting me on the back.

Afterward I watch for Mom. Then, across the street, I see Dad turning the corner, walking toward our favorite Chinese restaurant. I wonder if he's going there for dinner. He's walking slowly with his hands in his pockets. His head is down. He doesn't look like a violin breaker. In fact, he's not flitting here and there, moving fast like he usually does. His slow pace makes him look lonely, maybe even a little bit lost. I consider calling out to him, but instead I say nothing and watch him walk away.

Steam rises, along with the berry fragrance. Mom let me borrow her favorite bubble bath and I dumped half of the bottle into the water. It smells wild, like something that would grow in nearby Thatcher Woods, where Dad used to take Michael and me hiking when we were little. The outside edges of the mirror fog up as I step into the nearly scalding water. My muscles loosen, uncoil, and expand. I close my eyes and feel the quiet soothing me. I stay in the tub for a long time.

I open my eyes, realizing that the water is lukewarm now, but I don't want to get out just yet. The room's humid and my cheeks are sweaty, and it makes me remember going to Kauai. It was my favorite family vacation. Back when Dad loved his job and we took fun trips. Michael was in the fifth grade and I was in first. It was hot and muggy, and we were on the Pihea Trail. Fog was rolling in and out, and it took forever to hike that trail because Dad kept stopping us to tell us the names of all the plants and trees. Mom and I liked it, but Michael was getting impatient. He wanted to hike and see where the trail led, instead of stopping so much. But when I spotted a scarlet bird with black wings, Dad told me the name of it, too: 'I'iwi. When we finally made it to the edge of a cliff and felt the cool breeze, I saw the thick blue of the sky over the Kauai shore, and I felt proud to have a dad who was so smart.

In my room after my bath, I'm wrapping up in my fluffy robe when my cell rings.

"Can you talk?" asks Nick.

"Yes."

"Where are you?"

"I'm home—in my room."

"Guess what? I'll be in Chicago for Thanksgiving this year. With my dad."

Thanksgiving. Oh no. Will I have to spend the holiday with Dad?

"I was hoping maybe I could see you."

"You want to see me?"

"Of course. Who wouldn't want a date with a goddess?"

I'm so flustered that my words get all tangled up and I can't speak.

"Are you still there?"

"Yeah."

"I get in Wednesday. Want to go to a movie?"

"Sure."

"Are you sure you're okay?"

"Uh-huh, yeah. I'm fine. You were so nice to me, you know, while I was on the run. I really needed a friend and you were there. Thanks, Nick."

"No problem."

We hang up, and when I look in the mirror, it's good to see myself smiling again. Then I lie on my bed, stare at the ceiling, and plan outfits for our date. After doing this for a while, my thoughts bounce back to Nick. I wonder how he managed to pull it together so quickly when his parents suddenly got divorced. My family's only been split up for four days and already it's way too crazy. And Dad sure didn't plan too well, breaking my violin and screwing up our Thanksgiving.

I set my alarm for school tomorrow and turn out the light beside my bed. When I turn on my side I miss Calliope, who usually sleeps on my pillow right beside my head. It's strange not hearing the lullaby of her purring.

Dad reaches for my arm and softly says, "What's up?"

I turn around then, and when I see his head tilted, I remember how caring he really can be. He puts his arm around me and leads me into the living room. We sit down on the couch.

"Have a bad rehearsal?" he asks.

"Yeah," I whisper.

"A rehearsal on your birthday should be good," Mom says, sitting on the other side of me.

"I guess thirteen's bad luck."

Dad moves himself away and apart from me. He's staring across the room, and then asks, "What's your orchestra rehearsing?" His voice sounds like he's supposed to ask.

Still, I'm happy because he hardly ever asks me about the violin.

"Bach," I say.

He nods and stares at nothing.

"Tell us," Mom says, looking at me.

I sigh. "The conductor isolated the first violins. And then he picked us apart."

Dad rubs his arms like he's chilly, then wraps them across his chest.

"The shifts are difficult. Makes it almost impossible for us to play it together."

Dad fidgets and begins rocking back and forth. Then he stops rocking and does a few neck rolls.

"I missed the shift and he stared at me through the whole passage."

"Oh dear," Mom says. She slowly rubs my back as Dad stands up and starts to pace back and forth in front of us. Mom pats my leg. "Next time will go better."

"Aren't you going to say I should've practiced more?" I ask Dad.

"I think I'm going to faint," Dad says.

"Honey, what is it?" Mom jumps up and moves over to him. "Sit down. Put your head between your knees."

Dad slumps over. After a while, he gradually sits up. His face is flushed. He rubs his chest and says, "Okay," while staring off at nothing. "That's better."

Mom pats him on the shoulder. "You should get your-self checked out."

I let out a sigh, relieved he didn't pass out. I'm especially glad he didn't start yelling that I don't practice enough.

"Thought I was over that," he says.

"You've had this before?" Mom asks.

"Went away after I informed the old man I was switching from the violin to tennis."

"What?" Mom asks.

"Never mind. It's not important. I'm okay now."

31

Sleep doesn't know where I live. Memory after memory, turning and shifting, keeps me awake. Nothing I do—deep breathing, counting sheep, hiding under my pillow—none of it stops the movie threading through my mind. It's 4:15 a.m. and I feel like I've run a lot of laps. I get a drink of water and then go back to bed. I close my eyes. If I could play the violin it would help. But that would make Mom really mad so instead I put in my earplugs and listen to Joshua Bell.

My alarm goes off at six, blasting through the sounds of Joshua playing Brahms. I get out of bed and feel like crap. Then I run to the bathroom, lift the toilet seat, and vomit.

"What's the matter, Cassie?" Mom asks from the hallway.

When I emerge holding my stomach, she puts her hand to my head. "You're clammy."

I get a whiff of her perfume and my stomach tumbles.

"Get back in bed." She takes my elbow and guides me. "I'll call school and tell them you're sick." She covers me up, says, "And I'll make you some chamomile tea." She leaves the room.

In bed I don't feel very good, but I'm happy not to face my classes today. In my sleep-deprived state, none of it seems important anyway.

Mom sets down a cup of tea on my nightstand, and then sits at the end of my bed. She's dressed for work in a silk suit, her small hoop earrings shining against the blond highlights in her sculpted hair. "I'm going in to the office today but I'll try to get out early."

"Won't there be hell to pay?" I sit up in bed.

"Don't swear." Mom stands to fluff the pillows behind me.

"But that's what you always say. You know—when you have to go in on weekends." I take a sip of the tea. It's hot and tastes like flowers.

"I see I need to watch my mouth." She sits back down.

"But Mom, you haven't been there all week, and now you're saying you might leave early?"

"This is not something for you to worry about." She pats my feet. "Leave that to me. Finish the tea, then try and get some rest." She kisses me on the forehead, like when I was really little.

I sip the tea, so glad she isn't making me go to school. Yesterday I wanted to be there, but now my head is full of too much stuff and I can't take in any more details. Especially stupid ones. I never used to think school was stupid, but after everything that's happened, it all looks different to me.

I slip back down into the covers, and sleep and sleep and sleep.

Slam! A door closing rattles my wall and startles me. I sit up. What if it's Dad? I run out of bed, trip on the sheet, unwrap it from my foot, and dive at the door, locking it as fast as I can.

I listen with my ear against the door, trying to identify if the steps I hear on the stairs are in Dad's rhythm.

Then, three knocks on the door. "Cass?"

"Michael?"

"Yeah. Can I come in?"

I slowly unlock and open my door. "I thought you weren't coming until tomorrow."

"Hi, big brother!" Michael says sarcastically, imitating my voice. "Thanks for borrowing your friend's car and coming home a day early."

I laugh, standing on tiptoes to hug him.

"That's more like it." He says, patting me on the back.

I sit down on my bed.

"You look like hell, Cass."

I throw a pillow at him.

He sits beside me. He looks a lot like Dad, except he's

the calm version. But he has the same brown hair, only shorter; same blue eyes, only happy. "Are you okay?" he asks.

"I think so."

"You know what you need?"

"What?"

"A really special breakfast."

"IHOP?"

"Michael's."

"Since when can you cook?"

"I'm dating an older woman. She's been teaching me a thing or two."

"How old?"

"Twenty."

I start laughing.

"You already look so much better." He pats my knee. "C'mon, I've been driving all night and I'm starving."

I put on my robe and head downstairs, where I smell butter melting in the skillet and hear the coffeemaker gurgling. Michael's dipping pieces of bread into an eggy mixture, then flinging them into the frying pan. He has the big bowl, the sugar and flour canisters, a carton of eggs, and the milk spread out across Mom's showroom kitchen. Measuring spoons are turned on their side, dumping out bits of spice. Seeing the batter splattered on the flour-dusted counter makes me feel like I'm at Winnie's. Mom would have fits if she showed up right now. She's a clean-as-you-go kind of cook, and likes to keep her kitchen spotless.

I pour us some juice. The French toast browns, making the kitchen feel warm. I set the table with Mom's new dishes from Williams-Sonoma. I even add the matching cloth napkins. Michael heats the syrup in the microwave. "Nice touch," I say.

He's in the flow and doesn't reply. Just continues working, lifting out the French toast and serving it onto two plates. He even sprinkles on powdered sugar.

"I think I like this girlfriend," I say, after tasting the first bite.

"Melanie's great." He pours himself some coffee.

"What's her major?"

"Me." He takes a bite, them smiles with his mouth closed, his cheeks bulging.

"Very funny."

"Anthropology."

"Interesting."

He stops eating, puts his hands in his lap, and looks directly into my eyes. "Look, Cass, I'm really sorry. You know, about your violin."

"You were right about the evasion plan. I should've followed it better."

"Hey, don't blame yourself."

"I didn't see it coming."

"Neither did Mom or me."

"Looking back, I should've. First it was Mom's vase, then his computer. Makes sense that he'd wreck something of mine next."

"Not really. What doesn't make sense is why you went to see our grandfather." He resumes eating.

"I just thought he should know what happened to his violin. I thought he deserved that much."

"Waste of time, right?" Michael says, balancing a knife on the end of his finger.

"Why do you say that?"

The knife falls out of his hand and plunks onto the table. "C'mon Cass, when we were little, Grandpa always treated you like royalty and me like I didn't exist."

I look at him and let out a sigh.

He holds his cup toward me. "You were the queen because you played the violin. No room in his world for anything else—especially not sports—and definitely not tennis." He takes a sip of coffee.

I set down my juice. "What are you talking about?"

"When I got my first racket I showed it to him—uh, tried to show it to him is more like it."

"And?"

"And he told me, 'Waste of time. Be like your sister. Play the violin.' And then he tried to bribe me. He said he'd get me a rare violin if I gave up tennis."

"You never told me about this," I whisper.

"There was nothing to tell. I wasn't giving up tennis."

"He must've been really hard on Dad."

He gets very still. "I'm amazed you care—after what he did."

"He apologized."

"That's something, coming from him, I guess." He scoots back from the table.

"Mom's seeing a therapist. Do you believe it?"

"I'm not surprised."

"You always defend her," I say.

"And you always criticize her," he says. After a pause, he smiles. "Hey, hey, let's not start arguing, too."

I nod. I move the sugar bowl out of the way, and slide the saltshaker right next to the pepper so they're touching. "Thanks for coming home."

"No problem, sis."

Michael thinks the house feels weird without Calliope and drives me to pick her up at Debra's.

When we arrive, Calliope's asleep beside Debra's little boy on the couch.

"Oh, baby girl," I whisper, walking toward her.

Calliope stands up and stretches out her calico coat.

Debra's little boy smiles at her.

When I'm at her side, she lurches up to get her head petted.

He giggles.

I lift Calliope and cradle her in my arms like an infant, kiss her on the head, and then sit down with her in my lap. I look closely at her face. The pencil-thin scratch just above her right eye is almost faded.

Debra's son leans over and pets her head. It bobs up and down.

"Calliope's going back to her own house, Ben," says Debra. "Remember our talk?"

"She can live here," says Ben.

"You like her, huh?" I ask.

He nods his head yes and as he does, big tears start to flow down his cheeks.

"I'm sorry," I say.

Debra rushes in and lifts Ben up, carries him over to a chair, and holds him on her lap. "Oh, sweetheart. You got really attached to her, didn't you?"

"Don't let her go." He turns his head into Debra's shoulder and cries full throttle.

I'm almost crying, too, because I know what it's like to be without her. "You can come visit her anytime you want, Ben," I say.

"Shh, shh," Debra coos. "We can visit Calliope soon, right Cassie?"

"Definitely." I look across the room at Michael. He's leaning against the wall near the door, looking like he needs a road map to navigate us out of this situation. I take a chance and ask, "Ben, would you like to help me put Calliope in her carrier?"

"Can you show her where it is, Ben?" Debra asks.

He's still crying, but Ben slides off Debra's lap and leads me through the house to a room off the kitchen. The carrier is in the corner and he sniffles as he leans down and unlatches the door. I put Calliope inside and he shuts the door. "Thanks, Ben. I hope you come over to visit real soon."

He sniffles. "Right now!" He runs toward his mom. "I want to go live with Calliope!" he wails.

Debra pulls him close.

I head for the door. "I'm sorry, Debra."

She motions for me to keep going.

I carry Calliope out, taking the front stairs in quick, short steps. I know exactly how Ben feels.

At the grocery store I cut through the empty checkout line, turn right, and pass by flowers, chocolates, and greeting cards. At the end of the school supply aisle, I run into Dad.

In one smooth motion, I turn around and head back the way I came.

He grabs my elbow, "Wait."

I stop. I expect him to yell, but when I look into his eyes, he seems sad and worried. Maybe even worried about me.

"How's it going?" He lets go of my elbow and looks around.

I avoid his eyes and shrug.

"Look, Cassie." He shifts the pack of bottled water he's carrying. "I know you saw the old man. We should talk. Would you go over to Starbuck's with me?"

"Uh, no. I can't." I put my hands in my pockets.

"Is your mother with you?"

"No. I'm with Michael." When I look up at him, that's when I notice the difference. He's not jittery anymore, and his jaw's not clenched. He's calm. It's like his whole face is smoother, like something's been released.

"Michael's home?"

"Yeah, he's waiting for me. In the car." I rub my hands together, back and forth, nervous that he might head out there. I don't want him anywhere near Calliope.

"He could join us."

"I can't." I step back and brace myself for his temper, but he doesn't react the old way.

"Okay, Cass. Okay. But soon—let's talk, please."

"I have to go." I speed toward the door. I'm almost outside when I remember I didn't get the cat food. So I go back to the pet food aisle, hoping to avoid running into Dad again. I don't even read the labels; I just grab a few of the nearest cans, go through the express line, and get out of there as fast as I can.

When I sit down in the car, Michael's leaning over to pet Calliope through the metal bars on her pet taxi, which is perched on the backseat.

I slam the door. "Shoot." The door clicks as I open it and step back out.

Michael stops petting Calliope and shifts toward me. "Where are you going?"

"Dad's in there," I say, leaning into the car.

"You don't look so good."

"I forgot the litter."

"You stay here. I'll get it."

I tell him what kind to get, and once I'm inside the car, I relock all the doors. I do a sweep of the lot watching for Dad, looking for his Jeep, peering first out of Michael's window, then through the front windshield, then out my own side of the car. I finally remember that we're in Michael's roommate's car, so it would be difficult for Dad to find me. But just seeing Dad in the store gives me the jitters all over again, and I have to do something to deal with my fear. That's when I remember the woman back at the church who prayed by lighting all those candles. So when Michael gets back, I ask if we can make a quick stop at a gift shop. He agrees and makes a right out of the Jewel parking lot.

In front of the store, I hop out, saying, "I'll be quick."

Inside I head straight to the candle section. I check out the price on the bottom of the tiny glass votive candleholders, then calculate whether I have enough money to buy four, with enough left over for votive candles. When I'm sure that I can afford them, I load four into my basket, then move on to the candles. I sniff one labeled "blueberry bliss," then take a whiff of "cranberry crazy." I try "rows of roses," "lavender lovely," and "home is where the heart is." Before I put that one back, I sniff it a second time, just to know what such a place is supposed to smell like. I end up taking four of the "strawberry summer," thinking that it will be uplifting to smell warm summer in the cold of November.

Back at the house, I set down the pet taxi inside the entrance and unlatch the door. Calliope walks out slowly, tentatively. She lowers her head to sniff the floor, then stops and looks up at me. "Welcome home, baby girl." I lean down and stroke her head. She takes her time exploring, and every few steps, she stops and sniffs. Michael and I watch her check out the hallway, and then I follow her as she roams into the kitchen and sits in front of her dish. She looks up at me and this time I move quickly, wanting to make up for that other fateful night when I'd been oblivious to her hunger.

After I watch her eat every last morsel, I carry Calliope up to my room. When I put her on my bed, she strides to the pillow and gets cozy. I get the bag from the gift shop and Winnie's to-do list catches my eye from the corner of my dresser. I pick it up and see something small written at the bottom of the page, not listed in the "violin" or the "school" category. Upon closer examination, I see that it says, "Move litter box to basement."

That's when I realize that now, with Dad out of the house, I no longer need to worry about Calliope's safety. I carry the box to the basement, clean it, and return it to the same spot as when Calliope first came to live with us. Then I go up to my room and take her down to the basement, putting her in the box so she'll know where it is when she needs it.

Back upstairs, I clear off the top of my dresser. Then, one by one, I move my collection of glass violins from the dresser to my desk. When the space is empty, I go downstairs and lift a table liner from Mom's linen drawer and arrange it on top of my dresser. Then I put the violins on top of the liner and the glass candleholders among the violins. Unwrapping the scented candles, I sniff them before placing each one in a glass. After all the candles are in their holders, I stand back and admire my new violin goddess altar.

It's a start, but something's missing. I run downstairs

and find a small box of matches, then hurry back up the stairs. I light each candle, then begin rearranging things, moving a few violins back and several candles forward. The tiny flames flicker. I turn out the overhead light and sit on my bed. Glimmers of light twinkle off the mirror and capture the reflections on the glass violins. The flames whisper, almost like breaths. I close my eyes, then pray:

Goddess, wherever you are, help me to be strong. I want to stop running from Dad. Help me to find the courage to face him.

I open my eyes, hoping, wanting to see a goddess. But above the flames in the mirror, all I see is my own face.

35

Friday, Winnie's sister, Monica, drives us to school. As always, she's got the radio turned way up and she's singing along.

Outside it's snowing, making the sidewalk look like white velvet. I'm shaky as I make it to the front door. In the lobby, Rosa waves and comes over to us. "Are you feeling better?" she asks me.

That's when I figure out that Winnie told people I'd been sick. "A little," I reply, as I look around at all of the other students. Nothing has changed for any of them.

At my locker, I move books around and stuff the ones I need for the morning into my backpack. The morning passes, and on my way to third-period English class I'm surprised that it really feels okay being here, going on with my everyday life. If I just stick to the schedule and go through the motions, maybe everything will feel normal, as if my violin's not wrecked and Dad hasn't had to leave the house. Maybe it could feel like nothing has changed.

I eat lunch with my CYSO friends in the cafeteria. Winnie and I don't let on that my violin's destroyed. Even when the subject of the spring concert comes up, we talk about it like we'll both be there. Of course, Winnie will be there. But I know my violin can't be repaired, and I can't imagine getting a new one, so I don't know how I'm going to get back to the stage and perform with this group ever again.

Winnie suggests we all get together for something fun next Wednesday night, since it's the start of Thanksgiving break. She sets off a debate about whether everyone should go to the movies or get a pizza and rent a video at her house. After a discussion about which movies are playing at the Lake, the group agrees to meet at Winnie's house at seven.

Winnie bumps me in the rib with her elbow. "You in?"

"Umm, well—" I stare down at my tray.

"C'mon, Cass, it'll be fun."

"I can't." I fake needing to get something out of my backpack at my feet, because I can't look at her. "I have a date."

"What?" Winnie leans over and looks down into my face. "You never told me."

My face burns red. "I know, I know." I look over at her. "I've been sick, remember?"

"Who're you going out with?" She's not looking at me as she hisses this question. "Not Kurt, the violinist?"

"You don't know him. He's not from here."

With that, Winnie balls up her trash, yanks on her backpack, grabs her tray, and leaves. Everyone at the table pretends to be busy eating lunch, like it's the best meal they've ever eaten. But I know Winnie's not just mad that I didn't tell her about my date with Nick. She's also pissed that I didn't tell her right away, and especially that I didn't tell her *first*, before the others instead of at the same time.

"Win, wait!" I grab my backpack but leave my tray behind. I walk quickly to catch up to her, and when I do I plead, "Winnie, I was going to tell you."

"When?" She keeps walking.

"I've kind of had a lot of stuff going on." I shift my backpack and try to keep up with her.

"You used to tell me everything." She stops, crosses her arms, and glares at me. "No matter what!"

The bell rings and she heads toward her locker.

"Listen," I grab her elbow, and when we stop and look at each other, I realize she's more hurt than angry. "Could I come over after school to talk about this?"

"If you think you have the time."

"Yes, I have the time."

"Fine." She walks off ahead of me, even though we have a class together next period.

After that episode, my concentration is shot and I sit through the rest of my classes in a fog. I make sure to write down the homework assignments, but between doing that, I tune out and roam through a landscape of random thoughts. I wonder how Dad can go back to work, just like that, as if nothing's happened. Thinking about it makes me feel antsy and I shift in my seat.

I move on to the memory of Nick's brown eyes. The music in his voice. I ponder the reason I didn't tell Winnie about him right away. It probably sounds really stupid, but I think it's because I didn't want to share him with anyone yet. I still don't. But now that she knows, I don't feel like he's all mine anymore.

After school, Winnie and I walk to the car together but we don't talk. She's probably as relieved as I am to find Monica waiting for us. And Monica talks the whole way home, buying me time before the big discussion with Winnie. She drops us off on her way to the mall.

In the kitchen, Winnie offers me a glass of milk and some Oreos, so I figure she's not as mad as she was at lunch. I follow her up to the attic, where she shares a huge yellow bedroom with Monica. The frames of the three windows are trimmed in periwinkle. It was Winnie's idea to paint the beams sloping across the ceiling in a bright red V.

Their room always looks like a slumber party in progress. As usual, their beds aren't made. Clothes are off the hangers, strewn over desk chairs, and thrown in piles on the floor. Monica's guitar is lying in an open case in one corner of the room. Win's upright cello stands beside it. Something about the high ceiling and expanse of the room makes me feel like I can really breathe here.

"His name is Nick Ortiz." I sit down beside Winnie on the floor and put my glass of milk beside me.

She leans against her bed. "Where'd you meet him?"

"In the train station that night I ran away." I dip half an Oreo into my glass of milk, then pop it into my mouth.

"You met him almost a week ago and you never told me?"

"Things have been crazy—remember?"

"But you had time to get to know him, at least enough to make a date."

"Winnie, I'm sorry I didn't tell you." I shift to sit cross-legged, facing her. "It's stupid, I know, but after losing my violin and my cat, I wanted Nick to be all mine, so I kept him a secret."

"That's exactly what's bugging me. You haven't told me anything about being on the run."

"I'm not exactly proud of it." I sip the last of my milk.

"But you're keeping stuff from me, like we're not best friends anymore."

"Look—I didn't exactly take an amazing vacation or something. It started out okay—I mean, I met Nick right away. But then I got robbed, and then chased down by this yucky Vietnam vet hippie guy. I kept calling my grandfather, who wasn't home. It turned out he was in the hospital. But I didn't know, so I had no choice but to go to a homeless shelter for teenage girls."

Winnie pulls her knees up and wraps her arms around them. "I didn't know," she whispers. "What was it like—you know, out on the street?"

"It was scary. And kinda boring. There was no place to go and I had no money. The worst was I didn't know when

I'd get something to eat again." I push my hair behind my ears and think of Rachel and Jessica from the shelter.

"How'd you survive?"

"This might sound nuts, but when I played that hippie guy's violin on the street, I felt this inner power, a force, like maybe I actually had channeled a violin goddess."

"Goddess power, yes!" says Winnie.

"Am I making sense?"

She sits up straight. "Definitely. Goddesses are a divine source. It makes sense that you'd connect to one when you were doing something creative—you know, by making music." She stretches out her legs. "We discussed it at my church youth con."

"Youth con? What's that?"

"Youth conference. Back in October." She puts her hands together like she's going to pray. "Goddesses are about creativity, nurturing, and healing the oppressed." She nods at me.

"I've been hoping to get that feeling of power back— you know—from the goddess or whatever. After what my dad did to my violin, well, I've been feeling more scared, more unsure. What's keeping me going is thinking I'll feel strong again, if a goddess helps me."

Then I tell her about the homeless shelter, about my grandfather being so obnoxious and weirding out on me, and how he threw me out into the night. I tell her about finding a purple church, about the lady inside who showed me how to light the candles, and about coming home and making my own goddess altar.

Winnie asks me lots of questions, like she's a reporter

doing a special story or something. She asks what I thought about the shelter.

"It made me sad to see so many girls our age without a family or a place to live."

"I never think of kids our age being homeless. Only older people. You know, like that strange-looking guy who always asks us for money outside of Borders?"

"There were eleven other teenage girls in the shelter the night I was there."

"Oh, Cass, I'm so glad you're back." She leans over and hugs me. Then she stands and drags the blankets off her bed. "So tell me everything about Nick." She hands me a furry red blanket.

"He used to live in Chicago—in Lincoln Park. His dad still does." I follow Winnie's lead and wrap the blanket around me like a shawl.

"Did his parents get divorced?" She sits back down, facing me.

"Yeah. Now he lives with his mom in Iowa."

"So he's spending Thanksgiving with his dad and he asked you out?"

"Exactly."

"And Jeannine's going to let you go out with a total stranger?"

"That's the problem."

"Oh my God! You mean she doesn't know yet?"

"No."

"Now I don't feel so bad." She nudges me on the knee with a grin.

"You have to help me, Win."

"What are friends for?" She begins to laugh. "You're the only person I know who would run away and meet Prince Charming."

I laugh, too, and soon we're both giggling. And I know she's not mad at me anymore.

"Oh Win, he's soooo cute."

"Details—spill—I want all the details."

"He's really cool—his hair's really short, and it looks nice. He's about the same height as Michael. And he's got really great eyes—brown—like he's really seeing you when he looks at you."

"And?"

"And he's sweet. Really sweet." I tell her how he gave me his phone number right after I told him about Dad and the violin. And how he kept tabs on me until I got home, and that he asked me out as soon as he found out I was back home.

"I don't know what I'm going to do about this date though, Win. Mom has a fit every time I leave the house now after my little 'trip,' and I think she'll go nuts when she finds out about my date with this guy who doesn't even live here."

"I noticed that Jeannine's on high alert. When we dropped you off at Miss Sinclair's, she told me she was thinking of going back after she dropped me off so she could sit out front until you came out."

"I might have to sneak out because I'll die if I don't see Nick when he's here."

"Wow. You've got it bad, girl."

"You have to help me with Mom, Win."

"Wait—you're not calling her *Jeannine* anymore."

"No. She's really changed. I ran away, but it's like my mom's the one who's come back home. She's really there for me now."

"Wow. I'm really glad. Okay! So let's figure out a plan to get her to let you go out with Nick." She gets out a notepad and numbers the steps, one, two, three. Beside number one she jots down: "talk to Mr. Ortiz"; and number two: "Mrs. Ortiz"; and number three: "Nick." When she's got it all down on paper, she titles it "Operation Date." Then with a flourish, she rips the page out of her notebook, hands it to me, salutes, and says, "Good luck, lieutenant."

37

I don't get it—why do I have to take out the trash when Michael could do it? I always do it. Now that he's home, he could take a turn and give me a break. But Mom doesn't buy my argument so I march out to the alley and heave the garbage bag into the big green container. I make another trip there, then another out to the blue recycling bin.

On my way back I hear a bird chirping. It's so rare in November that it catches me off guard. I look toward the sound and high up on a naked branch I see a cardinal, bright red against a milky blue sky. The cardinal hops up. Through the branches a pattern in the sky catches my eye. I move out from under the tree to get a wider view. What I see is so profound that it scares me a little and almost takes my breath. I have to look away. I glance back again to make sure I'm truly seeing what I think I'm seeing. And sure enough, etched in the clouds is a flame, and inside it is a female shape, her arms raised up, her body floating in blue space. Maybe I'm crazy, but what I'm seeing looks a whole lot like a goddess to me.

The branches flutter just a little, just enough to raise

the goose bumps on my arms. I cross them, stand there, and stare. One of the goddess's hands is above the other, and both are cupped and reaching, as if she's expecting something—maybe a violin to drop from the heavens.

I have no words for the feeling that's filling me; it's coursing through my being, warming me on this chilly day. Somehow I know she's there, watching over me.

I slowly walk backward to the house, looking up at her all the while. The clouds move and her form dissipates from the sky but not from my heart. When I get inside, Mom says, "Thanks, Cassie. It's nice to see you being positive, especially when you're taking out the garbage."

I shrug.

"Got a minute?" She's leaning against the counter in the kitchen.

"What's up?"

"I want to let you know that I'm having dinner with your dad Sunday night."

"Oh."

"Let's sit down for a few minutes." She motions toward the table. "What do you think about it?"

"Does it matter?" I ask, sitting down across from her.

"Yes, Cassie, it really does." She clasps her hands, resting them on the table.

"If I say I don't want you to go, will you stay home?" I ask.

"I didn't say that." She adjusts the back post to her earring. "But I do want to know how you feel."

"I think it's too soon. And Mom, why do you want to be with him? You know—after everything he's done."

"Your dad's psychiatrist suggested that we have a date. She wants us to start thinking about whether we have anything left to salvage."

"That's weird."

"What is?"

"You and Dad—going on a date—it's weird because you're already married."

She smiles. "I know. It *is* kind of strange. But it's important to me to try to work things out with your dad, so I've agreed to go out with him."

"Do you actually want to go out with him?" I tilt my head to look at her, to really see her eyes.

She looks away. "Yes and no. Yes, I think it's a good suggestion. And I know it doesn't make sense, but I do miss him. . . ."

It's hard for me to hear this after what he did to me. "And no?"

"No because it's a little scary." She sounds uneasy.

"Will he come back with you?" I ask.

"No."

"Then I guess I'm okay with it. But I don't want to see him."

"Okay." She pats my hand. "I'm planning to meet him at the restaurant."

Since we're getting along okay, I decide to tell her about Operation Date. "Mom, can I tell you something?"

"Of course, Cassie. You can always tell me anything, no matter what it is."

"You know how I took the El to Union Station that night I left?"

153

"Y—e—ss." The way she draws out the word contradicts her readiness to hear what I'm about to tell her.

"I met a guy there."

"Oh?" She clutches the armrests on her chair.

"He's really nice—from Iowa. Well, he used to live in Lincoln Park. Before his parents got divorced."

"Have you been in touch with him since you got back?"

"Yes, we've called each other a couple of times. He's going to be here with his dad for Thanksgiving, and he wants to see me while he's here."

Mom pushes her chair back from the table. "This doesn't sound like a good idea to me. We don't know him or his family." She points to the tabletop. "It might not be safe."

"Oh, Mom, please. Chill out and just listen to me. His name is Nick Ortiz and he calmed me down when I was freaking out after Dad broke my violin and I lost Calliope. He really understood what I was going through, and even tried to talk me into going to Winnie's—instead of running away."

"He did?"

"Yes. He gave me his phone number and kept tabs on me the whole time I was gone. I want you to talk to his parents before you say no to us getting together."

"His parents?"

"Yeah. You know—so you can tell that he's okay—a good person. They're willing to talk to you," I plead.

She relaxes into her chair. "I suppose I could call them. But I'm not making any promises about letting you see him."

"He said they'll both be home tomorrow."

"Can I have their names and numbers?"

I get up. "His mom's name is Deirdre Ortiz. And his dad, I don't know. Mr. Ortiz, I guess."

"Cassie, why do you want to see him if he lives in Iowa? It's not like you can really date him if he's so far away."

I smile and struggle to hold myself back from gabbing on and on about how cool he is. "I want to see him again because he's funny and he's really nice, Mom. You'll see when you meet him—if you decide it's okay for us to get together."

Mom calls a family meeting, which isn't accurate, since it's not the whole family—just Mom and me and Michael at the table, without Dad. She's cooked Michael's favorite meal—lasagna—and she's set the table like it's a holiday, with a creamy linen tablecloth, the good china, and linen napkins. She lights the candles, then sits down and asks Michael to pass his plate. As she's dishing out a generous slice of lasagna she says, "We need to discuss Thanksgiving." Next she serves me, then herself.

"About that," Michael says. "I'm going to Melanie's—in some small town in Ohio—for the holiday."

"You are?" Mom passes the basket of crusty garlic bread to him. She eats her salad, reflecting on what Michael has just said, as if it's a difficult puzzle she's working out in her mind.

I put down my fork and fold my hands in my lap. "Is Dad coming back for Thanksgiving?"

She looks at Michael, then at me. "No. He wants to, but I told him that we're not ready for that yet. Besides, I've already made other plans." She sips from her water goblet.

"What exactly does that mean?" I take a bite of my lasagna.

"Debra's invited us to her house."

"Is Dad upset that he can't come home for Thanksgiving?" Michael asks.

"Yes, he is. We've never been apart before on a holiday and he doesn't want to spend the day alone." Mom concentrates on slicing off a piece of lasagna with her fork. "But we shouldn't force the issue and be together just because it's Thanksgiving, not after everything that's happened."

"Did he lose it when you told him?" I look at Michael.

"He was very sad, but reasonable—and calm." Mom starts to get teary. "He knows we all need time to trust him again. Especially you, Cassie."

This surprises me—to hear that Dad's being thoughtful instead of throwing things—and I drop my fork. But Mom misses my reaction because she's concentrating so hard on the small piece of garlic bread she's breaking off.

When I don't say anything, Mom asks, "Cassie, don't you want to go to Debra's?"

"I like her, but Winnie already invited me to spend Thanksgiving with her and her family." Mom is very quiet and doesn't reply, so I say, "I'd rather go there if it's okay with you. No offense."

Mom eats the last bite of her lasagna. I look over at Michael, who's busy mopping up the sauce on his plate with a chunk of bread. Mom wipes the corners of her mouth with her napkin. "Well, I don't like us going our separate ways on holidays. I'll miss you two. But I hope we'll all be together for Christmas."

"Definitely. Sounds like a plan," Michael says. "And next year'll be better, Mom. We'll be back together then."

Mom and I look at each other. I can tell from her re-signed expression that she'd like to feel as hopeful as Michael sounds, but she doesn't. Me either.

"How *is* Dad?" Michael asks.

"His doctor put him on medication." Mom stacks her bread plate and salad bowl on top of her dinner plate. "He has an anxiety disorder."

"A what?" I finish my last bite of bread.

"An anxiety disorder?" Michael asks, stacking his plates, too.

"What does that mean?" I ask.

"According to the doctor, anxiety can cause you to be so irritable and agitated to the point of becoming irrational, aggressive, and sometimes even violent," Mom says as she walks to the kitchen.

"Is his medication helping?" Michael asks. "I mean, does he feel any different?"

"He says he's sleeping a little better," Mom says, as she walks back into the dining room.

"Do you see any change in him?" Michael asks.

"I've only talked to him on the phone and at times he does sound calmer. But the doctor told him it could take a month for the drug to be fully effective."

I get up and collect my plates, but then I sit back down. My thoughts are racing. Does this condition mean it's not really his fault, his being so angry and breaking things? Does it mean he'll be coming back here to live with us? Will he be a normal dad when the medicine's working, or what?

When I hear Mom's heels clicking on the wooden floor, I stand up again, take my plates, and go to the kitchen.

"Are you okay, Cassie?" Mom asks, looking at me, searching for my reaction.

"I'm fine, Mom."

"You look a little flushed." She puts her hand on my forehead. "You're not coming down with something, are you?"

"Really, Mom, I'm fine. Relax, okay?"

We all make laps from the dining room to the kitchen to clear the table. Mom starts to load the dishwasher and asks about Michael's plans to return to school.

"I'll head out in the morning, Mom. Probably sometime around ten."

I gather the tablecloth up, keeping the crumbs inside. I step outside into the chilly night onto the top step and shake it out. The night sky has only two stars—they're just like goddess eyes. "I wish Michael didn't have to go," I say to her up there. And then I admit what I don't say out loud: It's a lot easier for me to go on with things when he's around. I'm really going to miss him.

I'm hiding outside Mom's home office because step one in Operation Date is about to happen and I want to monitor the situation. Mom calls Nick's dad first. She starts off sounding polite and cautious.

"Please, Mr. Ortiz, uh—Alex—try to see my point of view. I'm concerned because my daughter wants to go out with a boy who doesn't go to her school. And he doesn't even live in our town. We don't have any connections." There's a long silence and I wonder what Nick's dad's telling her. It surprises me when, after this long pause, Mom says, "You're kidding. Where's your office?" After he answers, she says, "Mine's right around the corner." He continues to talk to her and I don't know what he's saying but when she finally responds, she sounds a lot calmer. They go into a bit of chitchat, she laughs, and then they hang up.

"Cass, are you out there?"

Busted! "Yeah, I'm here." I get up from the floor and sit down on the loveseat in her office. She's still smiling, which makes me really curious about what he said to her.

"I assume you want every detail about my conversation with Nick's dad, Alex."

"Well, it couldn't have been too bad. You were laughing."

"If Nick's anything like his dad, I can see why you like him."

"What's that supposed to mean?"

"Nothing. Just that he's charming and very nice."

"What were you laughing about?"

"He admitted not being objective about his own son, and that he's crazy about him. He's pretty sure that when I talk with Nick, he'll manage to sell himself."

I smile. *Thank you, Mr. Ortiz!*

While I'm sitting there, Mom moves on to Operation Date: Step Two, and calls Mrs. Ortiz. This time I decide to camp out on the loveseat so it's easier to eavesdrop. Mom says, "I'm worried about my daughter going out with a stranger." Then there's a long pause, at which point she looks over at me and then replies, "Cassie's not a *runaway*. She's got some family issues that upset her, but she's come back to face them." They go back and forth for a while, talking about how Nick and I met. Then Mom listens for about five minutes, and then she responds by telling a little bit about me, saying that I'm a freshman in high school and a good student, and that I'm a soloist with the Chicago Youth Symphony Orchestra. By the time the conversation ends, they decide it's okay for us to see each other.

"And Nick's calling you today, too, right?" I ask.

Mom shifts around to look at the calendar on her desk. "Yes. Tonight."

When I don't get up to leave, Mom looks at me and says, "Is there something else you wanted to talk about, Cassie?"

"This is kind of nice." I lean back against the couch.

"What's nice?" Mom leans forward in her chair.

"Us—you know—working together on something. It's like having a project. . . ."

"Getting you a date is a project?" She smiles.

"Not really." I cross my legs. "It's just nice, us spending more time together."

Mom stands up, leans over the couch, and looks at her begonia plant on the shelf above my head. "I've been thinking we should do some holiday baking together." She breaks off a few dead leaves and then puts back the plant.

"But we're not having Thanksgiving here." I watch her as she throws the dead leaves into the wastebasket under her desk.

"It's a gracious thing to do, to take your hostess something homemade when you're invited to a holiday dinner." She sits back down.

"That'll be fun, Mom." I say, grinning. "We haven't made chocolate chip cookies since forever."

"Oh, honey." Mom takes a sip from her coffee mug. "I was thinking more along the line of pumpkin pies."

"But I miss your cookies, Mom." *And you being around.*

"Okay, it's settled then." She sets her mug onto the warmer on her desk. "We'll make pies for Winnie's and Debra's families. And we'll make cookies just for us."

I sit up straight. "Winnie'll kill me if I don't bring her some cookies."

Mom tilts her head. "I guess you can get away with it if you're also bringing a pie."

The cell phone in my pocket rings. When I answer it, Nick sounds worried. I start to think he's calling to cancel our date. He says, "Um, do you think I could talk to your mom this afternoon?"

"I'll check." I hold my hand over the phone and tell Mom what's going on, and she nods.

"The reason I want to talk to her sooner is that I forgot I have to work with my chemistry group tonight. We have a project due just before the Thanksgiving break."

"She's right here if you want to talk to her now."

"Oh. Right now? Yeah, okay. Let's do it. Please, put her on then."

I hand over the phone, wishing so bad that I could put him on speakerphone, but I know Mom wouldn't like it. I stay glued to the loveseat, thinking Mom'll wave me out of the room, but she doesn't.

"Nick?" Mom asks.

There's a long pause, like when she was talking to each of Nick's parents. I try to imagine what he's saying by reading her face for a reaction, but I can't tell. She's in her business mode, sitting up straight with her legs crossed, taking in every word. But she's also got her arm across her abdomen, like she's on guard.

I silently think, *Go, Nick, go*.

"If I were to say yes, what are your plans for the evening?" she asks him.

Poor Nick. She's put him on the spot, interrogating him.

I'm guessing he's telling her about our plans to catch a movie.

163

"And how would you get here?" she asks.

Oh brother, now she's expecting him to lay out all the details of our evening.

Whatever he's said prompts a compliment. She says, "Your folks seem like lovely people, Nick. And you seem nice, too. But I would feel a whole lot better about letting my daughter go out with you if you came here for dinner first."

And if he gets a D or an F for dinner behavior, then I can't go to the movies with him?

"Why don't you come over around 4:30 on Wednesday? We'll have an early dinner so that you two can make it to the show on time."

Then she says, "Nice to talk with you, Nick. I'm looking forward to meeting you next week."

She hands the phone back to me and I wave as I leave her office. I head up to my room and shut the door behind me.

"You must've done really well," I say. "She wants to cook you dinner."

"I guess that's something, right?"

"Do you even still want to go after all this?" I ask.

"Yep. Of course I do. Would I have gone through all this otherwise?"

I exhale. "I'm really glad. I guess I'll see you on Wednesday, then."

"Right. At 4:30, your house."

When we hang up I want to scream for joy, but I don't. Instead I go back down to Mom's office, lean over and kiss her on the cheek, and then leave.

There's a biology test tomorrow and I'll probably fail it. Maybe I could actually get a C, but that would mean I'd have to study all night. I haven't been able to focus since Mom left at six to meet Dad for dinner. It's too weird, my parents going out on a date.

I decide a change in position might help. So I gather my book, notebook, and study guides, then move from the floor to my bed. Calliope hardly wakes up when I move her off my pillow. After I'm comfortably settled, I get back to reading up on DNA, petting Calliope while I'm at it. It's no surprise when I get nine out of ten questions wrong on the practice quiz at the end of the chapter.

Frustrated, I decide to go downstairs. I never study there, but I feel like I need a change of scenery. I pour myself a glass of orange juice and set up shop at the kitchen table. Between sips I review my notes from class. At 8:30, I begin to feel desperate. I decide to try to memorize the answers to the questions on all the quizzes we've had, hoping Mrs. Reynolds will give me a break and put some of those same questions on tomorrow's test. By the time I take each quiz a third time, I get most of the answers right. I start to feel a little more confident when I hear the garage door going up.

I get up and look out the back door. I see Mom. Without Dad. I let out a relieved sigh. She'd said she wouldn't bring him home and I'm glad she kept her word. But when I go back to the table to gather up my books, I'm surprised to realize that I'd been hoping that, in just that one date, my parents would magically repair our family. I'd pictured things the way I wanted them, turning everything into any other ordinary Sunday night—the way it used to be before Dad became so angry. With all of us home together, gearing up to face another Monday.

Mom steps in from outside and right away I know that she's been crying. She tries to muster a cheery smile when she sees me, but her eyes don't let her lie. She says hello while dabbing at her eyes.

"Are you okay, Mom?" I pull out a chair for her.

She doesn't answer, doesn't even take off her coat, but sits down quietly, still all bundled up.

"I'll make some tea." I lift the kettle off the stove, fill it with water, and put it on to boil. When I turn back to my mom, she still hasn't taken off her coat. She looks kind of stunned.

"Was it really awful?" I sit down beside her and cover her hand with mine.

She doesn't answer right away. She keeps staring into space. Finally, she says, "No. He was on his best behavior."

The kettle whistles and I get up to make her a cup of tea. When I get back to the table, she's finally out of her coat. She whispers "Thank you" when I hand her the teacup.

I sit back down beside her and ask, "Was it weird, going out with him on a date?"

"It was strange. Obviously I know him really well. And yet, we're both trying to change. So it's like we don't know each other at all. It was sort of confusing." She takes a sip. "He seemed afraid to look at me at first, until I admitted feeling ashamed that I didn't realize what a hard time he's been having. Then he took my hand and held it for a long time. He used to always hold my hand when we were young. It was very sweet."

I fidget in my seat, because it's difficult to hear about my parents "dating," and it's strange that they're separated, too.

"Cassie, I brought up the subject of your violin."

"You did?" I look at her, wide-eyed.

She nods her head. "I told him that I think we need to do whatever we have to do to get you a new one."

"But what about the benefactor? It's special to be chosen."

She sets down her cup. "I don't think we have to decide about that right now, because as soon as I mentioned it, I could see that he's not ready to face it yet."

It hurts to hear that Dad's not jumping in to try and make it all better. But in a way, it's a relief. I'm really not in any way ready to accept anything from him—especially not a violin.

"It's even too soon for him to deal with talking about renting a practice violin." She looks at her hand, fidgeting with her wedding ring. "He still needs time." She looks at me. "Where you and the violin are concerned, it's a challenge for me to stand by and be patient, but right now I have to leave that subject alone when it comes to your dad."

"It's okay. I understand, Mom. I'm kind of relieved not to have to deal with it right now myself."

She clasps her hands and says, "You know, after I backed off, we actually got along okay."

"Really?"

"He wants to move back in."

I shudder. "Is he going to?"

"No. Not yet. But I hope we can work things out and he'll be able to come home eventually."

"Do you trust him? You know, to not be so angry anymore, and to not get violent?"

She raises her cup slowly, takes a sip, holds it for a few seconds, and then sets it down. "I want to," she says, staring out the window above the sink. Then she holds on to my hand. "But it's going to take time. Maybe a long time. He needs to work through his issues. And you and I need to be able to trust that he's stable. We both need to feel safe. Truly safe." She squeezes my hand very tight. "I'm never losing you again. Ever."

Maybe I'm in the wrong house. Or else I've morphed backward in time to when I was five years old. This is how I feel when Winnie and I get home after school on Wednesday and Mom's busy in the kitchen instead of still at work. Winnie's surprised, too.

Mom wipes her hands on a towel and asks, "How was school today?"

Winnie and I look at each other, not because it's a hard question, but because this is the first time Mom's ever been home at this hour.

"Um, fine. Just about every teacher showed a video today, since it's the last day before a holiday," Winnie replies.

I decide not to tell her I found out I bombed the biology test. "No one wanted to be there, the day before Thanksgiving," I add.

"I bet not even the teachers did," Mom says.

We laugh at this, and then Calliope strolls into the kitchen. I pick her up and pet her while Mom opens the cookie jar and takes out some of the cookies we baked last night, then arranges them on a plate.

"Mmm, those look so good," says Winnie. She reaches over and pets Calliope.

"Have a seat," Mom says.

"Didn't you have to work today?" I ask, setting Calliope down.

"I decided to take the day off today." Mom puts the plate in the middle of the table, gets the milk out of the refrigerator.

We chat with Mom and munch on cookies. It reminds me of what it was like when she didn't have her job. She'd pick me and Michael up from school, and when we got home the house would often smell of cookies. When I realize it's already 3:45, I jump up and announce, "I have to shower. Nick's going to be here soon."

"Would you like to stay for dinner, Winnie?" Mom puts the milk away.

Winnie looks at me, questioningly.

I think it's a good suggestion. "Nick'll probably feel a lot more comfortable if you're here, Win. I will, too." Besides, I'd like her to meet him and see what she thinks. "That's a great idea, Mom! Why don't you stay, Win?" I ask.

She smiles. "I did kind of want to meet Nick."

Winnie hangs out in my room, reading my new *Strings* magazine while I take a quick shower. When I'm done, she's got all the candles lit on my goddess altar, and my iPod's playing "Cowboy Take Me Away" by the Dixie Chicks. I slide open the closet door, then grab my favorite jeans and the camisole and crocheted sweater Win and I'd decided on last night. We sing the chorus of the song as I get dressed, then I blow dry my hair and style it so soft curls land on my shoulders.

Winnie does my makeup. She wants to use the new eyeshadow she bought when we went shopping last Saturday, but I hesitate when I see the colors. She reassures me that even though I have a lighter coloring, she'll be able to blend it so it works. First she brushes on the eyeshadow, then adds blush. When I look in the mirror, I'm surprised at how good it looks—not gaudy, which was what I'd been afraid of. I put on mascara, add lip gloss, recheck the mirror, and feel pleased that I don't look anything like that messed-up girl Nick met in the train station on that awful night.

Winnie says, "There's time for a quick goddess circle." She turns off the light and the room's shimmering in candle glow. I look in the mirror and smooth my hair once more. "Shoes! I forgot about shoes. Win, which ones should I wear?"

"Definitely your ballet flats." She turns the light back on so that I can find them in the closet.

I pose like the models do in *Seventeen*: head up, slightly tilted, shoulders back, hands at side, right foot out, casual. "What do you think?"

"It works. You look good enough for a magazine shoot!"

"Really?"

"For real."

My heart's beating wildly. "So what's a goddess circle?"

Winnie turns off the light again. "We did one at my

youth con. There were ten of us in the circle. I'll make one up just for us, okay?"

"Hurry. He's going to be here soon."

"Okay." She stands in front of the goddess altar, facing me. She takes my hands, saying, "Close your eyes."

I do, but it feels a little weird.

"I'm sending you light, Cass. Imagine yourself receiving the light."

Winnie's hands are warm. With my eyes closed, I feel this light glowing out of Winnie's head. I picture it arching up and over, and funneling into my head. In my mind, the room's no longer dark. Instead it's lit by this arc of gold energy flowing between Winnie and me.

After a minute or so, Winnie says, "We call to the goddesses and ask them to hear us today. The circle of light is now open." She lets go of my hands and I open my eyes. "Okay. At youth con, usually we'd sit down and each of us talked about what we'd asked for, but I think we should just stand here while I send up a few quick requests. Okay?"

I nod.

"Bring us peace and love. Especially watch over my friend, Cassie, out on her very first date." She lowers her voice to a whisper, explaining before going on: "Okay, okay, and this is what the circle leader said: 'Help us to be ourselves.'" She looks at me again, and whispers, "In other words, be real, girl," then goes on, "and Goddess, please keep her safe, wherever she goes tonight."

With that, the doorbell rings.

I gasp.

"Wait." Winnie grabs my hands. "We have to finish. It's important."

"Hurry!"

She closes her eyes and so do I.

"We thank all of the goddesses for joining us today."
Winnie gives my hands a squeeze. "The circle of light is
now closed."

I start to blow out the candles but Winnie stops me.
"Wait. Wait." She reaches out and hugs me. "Okay, now
you can blow out the candles."

Nick seems to jolt slightly when I enter the dining room. I guess I was right about looking a lot better than I did when he met me at the train station. His smile is big, like happiness is glowing out of him. He lets go of the chair he's leaning on and comes closer to me. I think he's going to hug me, but he only touches my shoulder. "Hey."

His voice alone makes me blush. Then I remember Winnie. I introduce them to each other and Mom comes into the room, carrying a crystal vase filled with spring blooms.

"Thanks again, Nick," Mom says, as she sets the flowers on the credenza.

I smile up at him. "They're gorgeous. That's so nice of you." I sit down and Nick sits beside me.

Mom motions for Winnie to sit across from me and then goes back into the kitchen.

"Do you play the violin, too?" Nick asks Winnie.

"No, the cello. But we're in the Chicago Youth Symphony together."

Mom returns and pours us each something to drink. After bringing in a serving dish with pot roast surrounded by potatoes and carrots, she sits beside Winnie and across from Nick.

"Help yourself." Mom passes the pot roast to Nick.

While we eat, Mom interviews Nick. It's like Winnie and I aren't even there, and we don't have any other conversation while she questions him. About Iowa, and his school. About the difference between living in Lincoln Park and in his new small town. She wants to know his favorite subjects in school, who his friends are, and what he does in his spare time. Once in a while, Winnie and I glance at each other. Mom grills Nick so thoroughly, I'm half expecting her to ask him something really personal, like if he's ever kissed a girl. But she doesn't, to my great relief.

When we're done with the meal and she's run out of questions, Mom finally asks us what movie we're going to see.

I'm so glad that the "interview" part of things is over, I actually let out a sigh of relief.

Nick tells her what we plan to see. And since his voice remains calm, it's hard to figure out what he's feeling or if he's as relieved as I am that the interrogation is over. "Well, we should get going," he says, getting up and beginning to clear his dish and silverware.

"That's okay, Nick. Just leave it," Mom says.

We're taking Win home on the way to the movie, and on the way out to Nick's Prius, Winnie gives me a high five. "Over and out, lieutenant. Well done."

In the car Nick asks, "What's that all about?"

We start giggling and Winnie fills him in on Operation Date.

"Thanks, I think."

I give him directions to Winnie's house and he pulls out of the driveway. At the light he glances at me. "Your mom's kind of intense."

Winnie starts laughing in the backseat.

"You think?" I start laughing, too.

"You handled her," says Winnie, "like a pro."

"Geez, I feel like I just got clearance from Homeland Security to take you out." He smiles at me.

After we drop Winnie off, Nick rests his right hand over the steering wheel and asks, "Where to?"

I check my watch. "The movie doesn't start for an hour."

"How about a tour? Even though I lived in Chicago, I've never been to Oak Park."

Mom's always taking people to the Frank Lloyd Wright Home, so I navigate us in that direction. It starts to snow and Nick puts on the windshield wipers. When we get to the house, the spotlights glow through the snow, showing off the triangular peaks of the rooftop. "Wow," he says.

Every few seconds the slow beat of the wipers interrupts the quiet, and the car feels cozy, like a very private room. I decide I like being alone with Nick.

"It's really nice to see you, Nick. I'm glad you came."

He stops looking out the window and glances at me. "Me too. It was worth jumping through all those hoops with the parents." He smiles at me. "Why don't you show me your school next?"

Passing restaurants and shops, I guide him through the

neighborhood to get to the school. Nick gasps when he sees that my high school spans an entire block. "You could fit two or three of my high schools in yours."

"I know what you mean. I only just stopped getting lost in that place."

Nick asks, "What's your favorite place in town?"

It takes me no time to decide where to go next, and I lead him back through downtown, into a different neighborhood. I tell him to take the open parking spot in front of the travel agency while I scan the area for Dad. It's deserted except for a few people going into the restaurant at the end of the block.

"I don't get it," he says. "What's so special about this part of town?"

I point to a window on the second floor of a building with a gold lyre etched on it. "That's my violin teacher's studio."

He leans toward the windshield to get a better look. "I'd love to hear you play, Cass."

"Maybe you will, someday."

He shifts to face me. "Did your dad get you a new violin yet?"

"No, and I don't want him to."

"Why not?"

"Because then the violin's about him. This time, I want it to be mine, free and clear of my family." I tell him about the benefactor, and that my teacher gave me one of hers to practice on in the meantime.

"But don't you miss your old one?"

"Nick, you have no idea."

"I know it's not the same, but if I couldn't go to the batting cages in the winter, I'd go completely nuts. I have to play baseball as much as I can."

"I'm hoping the goddess will help me—you know—help me figure out how to get back to the stage."

"You're still searching for a goddess?"

"Not just any goddess. A violin goddess."

"Well, I think I found mine." He leans over and pulls me into a hug. "I didn't expect you to be so pretty." He smells great, and the way he holds me—so strong and so gentle—feels really good. Being this close to him is divine. Then I think, *if this is just a hug, kissing him must be unbelievable.*

"We should get going, if we're going to catch the flick," Nick says. He lets go and I notice the windows have started to fog up. He switches on the defroster and when the windshield's clear, he pulls out.

At the movie theatre, we decide to skip the popcorn. Nick leads me to a seat all the way at the end of an aisle near the back. When we sit down he moves close to me and our shoulders are touching. After the last trailer, when the lights go down, he reaches over and takes my hand, resting our clasped hands on his leg. Warmth envelops my hand. I feel calluses on his palm, but the top of his hand is smooth. I try to focus on the movie, but all I can think about is how I love holding his hand, and that I love sitting next to him. I want to sit beside him like this for the rest of my life.

My fantasies of holding hands with Nick out in public weave in and out of the story on the screen. Then I wonder if he'll kiss me goodnight, and if I'll be able to do it right.

Finally I settle down and watch the movie, but by then I've missed so much that I spend the rest of the time trying to figure out what's going on.

Afterward, Nick says, "Let's get some hot chocolate."

I suggest the bookstore café and he takes my hand as we stroll down the block.

"How's it going—you know, with your parents being split up?" he asks, swinging my hand in his.

"It's rough. I'm trying to get back into things—you know, school, my violin lessons, the holiday—but it's weird." The spotlight in the optometrist's storefront glows on different pairs of glasses. "Everything's changed."

"It takes time," he says.

Suddenly I grab on to his arm and pull him into a doorway, getting behind him and making him my shield.

"Cassie, what's wrong?" He looks at me over his shoulder.

I watch the man across the street walking by the stationery store. I relax my grip on Nick's back. "Oh, it's not him."

"Who?"

"My dad." I grab at his hand and we start walking again. "I thought it was him."

Nick lets go of my hand and puts both of his on my shoulders and looks into my eyes. "Wow. You're a wreck again."

"I found out mine wasn't the first violin he broke." I say it to the ground, not to his face.

"You talked to him?"

"No. My grandfather told me. You know—when I went

to Pretoria. After I met you." I start walking again and Nick takes my hand again. "I'm still too afraid, to face Dad. To talk to him about how he's messed everything up with his crap."

"You seem very strong to me."

"That's the thing—I felt strong, playing my solo in front of all those people at my concert. But now, it's like I'm missing a body part—like my arm's gone. I don't feel like myself anymore without my violin."

He squeezes my hand. "When do you think you'll get a violin from the benefactor?"

"Soon, I hope."

Nick opens the door for me at the bookstore café.

Walking in, I tell him the worst part. "If I don't have a violin by January—when rehearsals start up again—the conductor's going to dump me."

"For real?" His eyes widen as he says this.

I nod as I lead him to the café in the back of the store.

Nick treats me to hot chocolate and makes sure it comes with whipped cream. We sit huddled together at a table in the corner. Outside it's begun to snow again.

"Thanks, Nick. This is way better than the kind of hot chocolate I had at the train station that night."

"I never thanked you for running away." He smiles at me.

I nudge him on the arm. "You're welcome. But enough about me. Tell me more about you. Like what's your favorite thing about playing baseball?"

"Batting. Definitely!" He swings as if he's holding a

bat. "All that force . . . it feels incredible to see the ball soaring way out there."

"I bet it would feel great to whack something," I add.

"You know what you need?" Nick asks.

"A new violin?"

"Batting cages."

"Excuse me?"

"Trust me. How about Friday?"

I smile that he's just asked me out again. "Friday works."

"I'll give you a quick hitting lesson and then you can bat in the cage."

The idea sounds totally crazy, and Miss Sinclair would not approve. But I'd go just about anywhere with him. "Sure. Sounds like fun."

When we get up and go outside, Nick grabs my hand right away. This time it feels like he's holding on to me even tighter, which I like. I feel really close to him right now and I hold his hand tighter, too. The wind is wild and other people are trying to walk quickly to get wherever they're going. But we take our time, like it's a calm spring day.

Once we're in the car, I give him directions back to my house. He parks in front, and when he turns off the car instead of making a move to get out, he leans toward me. I lean toward him, too, and he smoothes my hair back from my face, his fingertips brushing my right cheekbone. The tenderness of it makes me close my eyes. Next thing I know, he's kissing me. He has soft warm lips that feel like a gentle swirl.

"I had a good time tonight," he says.

"Me, too."

"See you Friday?"

"Definitely."

I wake up to the aroma of turkey at around eleven the next morning. It confuses me since we're not going to be home for Thanksgiving. And when I get downstairs, Calliope's at her dish, eating, while Mom's at the counter, peeling sweet potatoes for the casserole she always makes on holidays.

"What's all this?" I ask.

Mom stops working and turns to me. "When you don't host, you don't have leftovers." She resumes peeling into the sink. "This way, we'll have them anyway."

I pour myself some orange juice, thinking it doesn't make sense. "Great." I go back upstairs to shower. I guess Mom's the type who feels like she has to cook on Thanksgiving, no matter where we're going to eat.

Dressed, I head back downstairs. Through the tiny windows on both sides of the door, I can see that it's snowing pretty hard. I put on my black peacoat, then pull on my gray beret and the matching fleece mittens. When I look for my boots, I see the whole family's boots lined up together, like we're all still together in spirit. I get teary. It doesn't feel right to take my boots away from the others, so I leave them where they are.

Mom backs the car out of the garage, and when I get in, she yells at me for not wearing my boots.

As she drives off, I look out my window and keep silent, focusing on balancing the pie I'm holding in one hand and the plate of cookies in the other. We each stay quietly involved in our own thoughts all the way to Winnie's.

I arrive at Winnie's and once I'm inside, she introduces me to her aunt Lou, who's putting onion rings on top of a green bean casserole. Standing beside her aunt is Winnie's mom, who's dumping out water from a big pot of potatoes. She asks me how I am.

"We made these for you guys." I set down the pie and the plate of cookies on a side counter.

"Thanks, sweetie." She transfers the potatoes into a mixing bowl.

Winnie's two little boy cousins run through the kitchen and Win asks me to help her finish setting the table. She points to a tray of glasses and grabs a pack of napkins. We work side by side—me setting out glasses and Winnie putting napkins at each place. "Was your date really bad?"

"No, it was great. Why?"

"You look like you're in a bad mood"—she points to my left eye—"and your mascara's running a little."

I wipe away the smudge, look around, and when I see we're alone I whisper, "He kissed me."

She grabs my wrist and muffles a scream.

"We're going out again tomorrow." I smile.

"So then why are you crying?"

I set down the last glass, cross my arms, and shift away from her. "It's just weird. Not being with my family on Thanksgiving."

She rubs my arm. "I'm really sorry, Cass. But I'm glad you're here with us. It's great to get to spend a holiday with my best friend."

I hold back tears and reposition one of the glasses slightly to the right.

"Mom's totally been looking forward to you being with us today."

"Really?"

"Seriously. You know, sometimes I think she likes you more than me," Winnie says as she sticks her tongue out at me.

"Cassie! Happy Thanksgiving!" Her dad comes in and gives me a big hug, crushing me into his soft flannel shirt. He introduces me to Winnie's uncle Joe, who shakes my hand.

"Hey, Cassie, Happy Turkey Day," says Monica, Winnie's sister.

Win's mom comes into the room. "Bob—it's time to carve the bird!"

Winnie's dad claps his hands and heads into the kitchen.

Then she asks us to give her a hand, and Winnie, Monica, and I follow her into the kitchen. Mr. Williams is carving the turkey on the center island counter. Seeing him at work reminds me of Dad, who always carves our turkey. "Cassie—please grab the salad out of the fridge, will ya?" Win's mom says.

I follow them back and forth to the dining room a few times, until all the food is on the table. We all sit and say a short prayer, just like we do at my house.

Now the conversation bounces around to all the guests as the food is passed around the long table. I take a little bit of everything, and as I pass the dinner rolls, I flash back to Rachel and Jessica at the shelter, hoping that they're both finally back home. I watch Winnie's dad put food on his plate. He's only taken turkey and mashed potatoes, with the potatoes filling up most of his plate. I watch him push the potatoes into a perfect mound, anticipating his next move because Dad has this same ritual. Sure enough, he makes a careful indentation at the top of the mound, then pours gravy into it. As I watch the gravy flow down the sides of his mashed potato volcano, I begin missing my dad so much that I have to quickly begin eating to distract myself from my rapidly forming tears.

Meanwhile, around the table, each story that's told is light and easy. At my house, we're usually quieter and more serious on holidays, and hardly anyone laughs very much. Win's dad tells us a funny story about misdirected mail and I begin to cheer up. And the food's excellent. Having been on the street not too long ago, I'm especially grateful to have so much to eat. It's almost like I'm tasting Thanksgiving dinner for the first time and I finish everything on my plate.

Later, Winnie, Monica, and I clear the dishes while Mrs. Williams makes coffee. Winnie helps me bring in my pumpkin pie and the cookies, and Monica carries in a huge tray of brownies. Then she returns with two kinds of ice cream. Upstairs after dessert, Winnie and I lounge on the floor of her room, listening to the Celtic Woman. I'm flat on my back and so full from the brownie-cookie sundae Monica dreamed up that I feel like I'll never move again.

"You seem better, you know, than when you first got here," says Winnie.

I lean on my elbows to face her. "It's weird, Win. I actually miss my dad."

She sits up looking quizzical.

"It doesn't make sense, does it?" I look up at the ceiling, as if I might find a goddess up there.

"It actually does, a little." She crosses her legs at the ankles. "It shouldn't, after what he did to you, the cat, and your violin. But, I mean, it like does, because he's still your dad. And he wasn't always like this." She begins to swish her top foot to the slow beat.

"He actually said he's sorry," I whisper.

"You mean you talked to him?"

"Not really. He was waiting at the house the day I got home. I wouldn't get out of the car with him there, so he apologized through the window."

"Saying it is great. But what's he going to do, you know, to earn your forgiveness?"

I stare at the ceiling. That's one of the big questions of my life right now.

I wake up confused again. Am I at the shelter? But something smells familiar. I sigh, realizing it's Mom's air freshener. It reminds me of cake icing. I remember now— I'm in the family room. I couldn't sleep so I came down here out of boredom. I shiver and reach for Mom's soft throw, wrapping it around myself. My grandmother's old clock taps out tiny, breathlike minutes as it ticks. Sitting there, I wonder: *Will things ever get back to normal?*

In my fog, I stare at our family pictures on the mantle across the room. Something about the way they're arranged draws me close. In the one on the left, taken at last year's spring concert, I'm hugging my violin, and standing between Mom and Dad. I'm wearing a black silk sheath dress, which Mom loved and I hated because I could hardly move in it. Mom and Dad look like they just stepped off a movie shoot, with every hair in place. Dad's looking through the lens, but he's not seeing the photographer. I move to get a closer look at the Mangenot. The cherry lacquer of the highly polished varnish makes it look like a bloodstain against my dress.

Next is a picture of Michael and his tennis team, taken last June when he won the state singles tournament. He's holding his racket like it's a magic wand and he looks very at home on the court.

The next one, my favorite, shows the four of us in Kauai—our last real happy time together. We're standing at a lookout point, leaning against a fence. Variegated mountains—shades of brown and reds and sage—are in the background. I pick up the photo and study it. Dad's on one end of the group, with his arm around Michael. I'm next, with Mom's arm around my shoulder, her fingertips reaching out and touching Michael. Mom and Dad are leaning in close to us and our faces are flushed and sweaty. Mom's hair is frizzy, wild, and carefree. Michael's holding on to Dad's arm and it looks totally natural and unforced. I look content, nestled between Michael and Mom. We could be a travel poster for Hawaii: *Come here and be happy, just like this perfect family.*

When I set the picture frame back down on the mantle, something out of place catches my eye. It's a vase sitting on the small table next to Mom's latest issue of *Architectural Digest.* I've never seen it before. It looks delicate but when I pick it up, it's very heavy, a red cylinder etched with lotus flowers. I turn the vase in my hand, wondering how long it took the artist to etch each flower. It must be like making snowflakes. Did Mom buy it for herself? She's always been drawn to the intricate designs in Oriental art. It's like some part of her soul is Chinese.

When I look inside, I see a small piece of paper with a message in Dad's precise handwriting: *"Jeannine, I hope you can forgive me. I love you, Frank."* I sit down and hold the vase in my lap. It's exquisite. Dad must've spent a lot of time looking for exactly the right one. Maybe he even went to Chinatown to get it. This surprising gesture makes my leg muscles go weak.

Tears fill my eyes, and for the first time, I wish that my father would shop for me. I wish he would choose a violin that's perfect for me, just like this vase is so right for Mom. I set the vase down, put my face in my hands, and lose it.

"Don't stand by the window, Cassie," Mom says, putting her boots away in the hall closet. "You don't want to look too eager."

I drop the living room curtain and go sit on the steps. Eager is exactly what I am—eager to get out of the house before she asks Nick where we're going. Because if she knew we were going to the batting cages, she'd never let me go. Mom worries about my hands—about me hurting them and not being able to play. She obsesses about it even more than Miss Sinclair does. Even Winnie told me not to go.

But I really want to try it. And that's why I'm sitting here, sweating to death in my coat, waiting for Nick. I told Mom we're going to lunch. And maybe we will. I've brought enough money to treat him—just so I don't feel like a liar.

I know Nick's out front because I hear his car. I jump up, open the door, and shout to Mom in the kitchen, "Okay, Mom. Nick's here," and then, from outside, I yell, "See you later!" I slam the door and run, hopping into Nick's car before he has a chance to open his door.

"I would've come to the door," Nick says. He's wearing a blue fleece jacket and a Cubs cap.

"Next time, okay?" I smile at him as I put on my seat belt. Then I look back at my house. Good—no Mom in sight.

"I went online and found a batting cage nearby." He reaches for a piece of paper between the seats.

I take the directions and navigate. "Turn right at the corner."

"I didn't expect you to be this excited about going to the batting cages."

"Well, I had a lot of fun with you the other night," I say, looking out my window instead of at Nick.

"Yeah, me too."

Soon we turn into an industrial park and follow the signs to the end of the lot. Nick parks in front of what looks like a large warehouse. The sign on the door says "Home Run City." A guy my dad's age holds the door open for two little boys going inside. All of a sudden I feel a little weird. I know nothing about baseball, nothing! *What am I getting myself into?*

"Ready?" Nick asks.

"I guess so."

Inside, the vast space is divided into three long rectangular sections and there really are cages. They're made out of black netting, and beside the last one there's an open area that's carpeted in green to look like a grassy field. Every few seconds we hear a metal ringing sound that I don't recognize.

Nick buys us a bunch of tokens from someone at a

cashier's window. I notice that Nick's got a different kind of energy about him here, like someone who's in charge. He finds the entrance to the cages and opens the door for me. The ringing sound is much louder here, and it comes from the back corner of each cage when someone swings his bat at the ball. The place smells like the locker room at gym class, like sweat and stinky feet.

"I'll be right back," Nick says.

A guy my age is standing on a mound and pitching. Every so often he throws a ball, and the *thud* as it slams into his instructor's catcher's mitt echoes in the large space. Beside him are three more cages, and inside the cage on my right, a small boy waits for a pitching machine to send him a ball. He swings, misses, and repositions himself for the next ball while his dad watches behind him from outside the cage.

Nick's back. "Hey Cass, come on over here," he says.

I follow him around the corner to a wall lined with all kinds of metal bats in different colors and sizes.

"First things first." He pulls something out of his side pocket. "Put these on," he says, handing me a pair of black leather gloves. "They're made for batting."

I thank him, slide on the smooth gloves, and adjust the Velcro on top of my wrist. I wiggle my fingers, turning my wrist to check the fit.

"They'll protect your hands. I don't want anything to happen to them while we're here." He takes a red bat off the rack behind us and hands it to me. "Try this one."

It's lighter than it looks. I grip it in my gloved hands and hold it up to my face, like a mirror. "It's nice."

He smiles. "Swing it," he says, stepping a few feet back from me.

I start to get into what I think is the right position from watching the Cubs on TV with Winnie and her dad.

"Wait. Move your left foot forward a little."

After I adjust my foot and bend my knees again, he asks, "How's your balance?"

"Better."

"Great. Let me show you something else." He takes the bat and has me look at where he positions his hands on the black rubber handle.

I take the bat back and grip the handle, this time with my right hand above my left. Then he helps me move into position from close behind me, almost as if we're in a sort-of hug. He lowers my elbows a few inches and angles my bat down a bit. Being this close to him is making it way too hard to concentrate.

"Try this." He takes the bat again, steps back, and swivels his upper torso.

I take the bat and try to mimic his movements.

"That's it," he says. "Now, watch my lower body." In slow motion, he shifts his hips, moving his weight from his front to his back leg.

I do the same thing a few times and it feels like slow dancing.

Then he points at his feet and demonstrates the proper footwork. "First step left, then right."

I practice the steps.

"Now put it all together."

I take a deep breath and get into batting position. Looking at Nick, I lower my arms. I swing the bat at the air.

"How'd it feel?"

"If bats are like violins, this one's too long for me."

"How's the weight?"

"It feels okay."

Nick looks around for a shorter bat in the same weight. He hands me a gold metal one.

I take a swing. "This is it."

"Great."

I swing again.

"Trust your hands."

I breathe into the swing.

"Focus."

I take a stronger swing.

"You're getting it."

Nick gets a black helmet and hands it to me. It's lined with foam rubber, which makes it snug on my head. I like the heaviness of it. Violin Girl turned warrior, I follow Nick over to the entrance to the cage in the corner. "For your first time, you should use this cage. This machine gives you the slowest pitch—about thirty miles per hour."

He points at the other end. "Once I turn on the pitching machine, wait and watch for the ball." He lifts the netted flap for me and I go into the cage, then get into position. Outside, Nick drops a token into the coin machine against the wall. "Are you ready?"

"Aren't you coming in here with me?"

"No way!"

I turn back around and try to remember everything Nick showed me. It's scary to be in here by myself.

"Remember: look only at the ball and nothing else."

I stare at the machine. For a while nothing happens. And then I see it: a ball is moving up and it flies out of the opening. It comes at me fast, in an upturned arc, and before I have a chance to react, I've missed it. It's frustrating, but I wait and watch for the next pitch. Just like the first one, it flies right past me. And so does the next one.

"Hang in there, Cassie."

I get myself into the timing of the machine, and when the next ball flies out, I'm ready. I swing and miss.

I swing at the next one and the tip of my bat catches the ball, which shoots off to the side.

"That's it!" Nick shouts. "Way to get a cut!"

His cheering pumps me up.

The machine catapults the next ball upward. I swing and miss again.

I breathe out. While I watch for the ball, I think about what Nick told me to do: *Move the front foot out a little. Trust your hands. Focus.*

The machine shoots a ball. It soars, curves up, and I grip the handle, watching as it flies. I aim my bat, twist my hips and give it all I've got—violin-arm muscles working in a different kind of concert. I twist my wrists and *whack*! My arms vibrate as the barrel of my bat connects with the ball. It's up and out—and it flies away, soaring until it slams into the back wall of the room.

"Woo hoo!" I scream.

"Way to go!" Nick shouts.

The balls come one after another. I hit a bunch in a row, but none of them goes very far. And then I get it right once again, connecting metal to leather. And it's out of there. One after another after another, I'm connecting bat to ball, twisting, swinging and hitting home runs. I'm the most powerful Violin Girl in the universe. I feel like nothing can hurt me—not anyone, not even my dad. I no longer feel helpless. I'm not a victim. I'm no longer afraid—not of anyone or anything.

I feel like a hulk when I step out of the batting cage. The bones in my forearms are reverberating power, with lightning vibrations tingling up and down. My heart is racing and my breaths are uneven. Sweat drips out of my helmet and down my cheek—but I don't care. Hitting is like being all-powerful. Now I'm a true force.

I sit on a bench behind a seventy-five-mile-an-hour batting cage and watch Nick swing. He's fluid and nimble. And as he moves into the zone, his bat rings out a beat of hard-hit leather baseballs. That's when I get it: this place is a symphony center for baseball players. I clasp my gloved hands around my bat and absorb the happiness of this moment. I want to hold it tight for as long as I can.

Then we step outside, and I feel like light is flowing out of me, even though it's a cloudy day. I am like a shining sun.

"Let me treat you to lunch!" I say, getting into Nick's car.

"I had lunch before I picked you up."

"But we have to go to lunch."

"Why?"

"I told my mom that's what we were doing. You can't make me a liar now."

"I could go for a Blizzard."

"Then Dairy Queen it is."

He drives down the road and I swear I'm not sitting in the car. Instead, I'm actually floating to our destination.

Inside Dairy Queen, I order Nick a large chocolate Blizzard with peanut butter cups, and I get myself a cheeseburger, large fries, and a milkshake. Suddenly, I'm starving. When we sit down, Nick starts laughing as he points to my batting gloves. "You're supposed to take those off when you're done batting."

"Do I have to?" I tease. I rip at the Velcro on each wrist and pull the gloves off, setting them on the bench beside me.

"You should play girls' softball," Nick says as he digs for peanut butter cups with a long spoon. "You'd make a bunch of people happy." He shovels the chocolate cups into his mouth.

"I can't give up the violin," I say, smiling at him. "And I can't do both." I sip at my milkshake. "I practice three hours a day during the week. If I tried to do both, I'd have no time left for school."

"True." He digs out another scoop of ice cream. "Sometimes I can barely handle things during baseball season."

"I'd like to come to one of your games sometime." I take a bite of my burger.

"That could be arranged," he says with a grin.

I put down my burger. "I wish you lived here, Nick."

He stops eating and goes all quiet. Then, "That makes two of us."

"Why'd your parents split up?"

He looks into his cup and starts stirring. "We're having such a good time." He looks up at me. "Let's not ruin it, okay?"

"C'mon, you know so much about me. I hardly know anything about you."

"You got me there."

"So, what happened?"

"My dad met someone else." He shoves ice cream into his mouth.

"What do you mean?"

He takes a long time to swallow his ice cream. Then he says, "What I mean is, one day he just got tired of our family and left. He moved in with somebody else."

This stuns me. I don't know what to say. I thought breaking my violin was bad. "I'm sorry."

"It's okay, now. Mom still cries sometimes, but we're on track again. At least we are for the most part."

"And you had to move away?" I put the half-eaten pack of fries down on the tray and push it away.

"Yep. But I made varsity as a sophomore in the new school. At least that worked in my favor."

"You felt like playing, after all that?"

"For a long time, baseball was the only thing I still cared about."

I grab both of his hands and link his fingers with mine. I don't say anything, and we smile into each other's eyes.

He's amazing. Right up there with Brahms and Bach—and that's saying a lot for a Violin Girl.

My arms are sore from batting but I practice the violin anyway. I'm taking forever to get through a few bars because I'm waiting to hear from Nick. He's on his way to the train station and it's like I can literally feel him going away from me. He won't be back until New Year's Eve—it's his Mom's turn to have him with her on Christmas, so he won't be here. His dad gets to have him visit here for New Year's. I want him around for both, but there's nothing I can do about it.

I give up and put the violin away. I lie on the bed, move Calliope from my pillow to my side, and pet her while I stare at the ceiling. Last night, after Nick kissed me goodbye, he hugged me for a really long time. It was so cold outside, but I was warm inside his hug. I looked up at the stars to see if the goddess was there, sure I'd see her because I felt her energy. But she must've been hiding behind a cloud.

When my phone rings I answer it on the first ring. "Are you at Union Station?"

"Yeah, I'm at my gate." He doesn't sound happy.

"Are you okay, Nick?"

"Iowa's too far away," he says. "From you."

"I have an idea," I tell him.

"What's that?"

"It's probably stupid."

"Just tell me what it is."

"I was thinking I'd make us each a calendar. I'll email one to you. When you get it, print it out."

"Okay."

He doesn't sound too excited, but I go on anyway. "When you get it, my name will be on December 31st. All you have to do is circle it."

"That's a long way off. I'm not sure I'll want it staring me in the face all that time. It's more than a month."

"But wait. Every night before bed, we get to cross off a day."

"Okay."

"With each X, we'll be closer to seeing each other again."

It gets quiet, but we stay on the line, hanging on to each other in the only way we still can.

"Will you do it, Nick?" I ask.

"Yeah. And I'll find the fattest, reddest permanent marker to cross off all those long, gloomy days."

"That's the spirit."

It takes forever to hang up. Then I daydream back through each memory of our two dates and all the phone calls over the past weekend, savoring every second. I want this daydream to last until New Year's Eve.

I'm probably the only person on earth who likes Mondays. But that's when I have my violin lessons. That Monday after Thanksgiving, thinking about my lesson makes school go faster. When the final bell rings, I'm one of the first of us out the door. A quick walk and I'm there at the studio, ready for my lesson.

Miss Sinclair opens the door, all excited. "Good news! The Stradivari Society called—they've got a lender who's just bought a special violin. And you're a potential recipient!"

"Great!" I try to catch my breath as I follow her inside.

"A representative's bringing it from Vienna in mid-December." She sits on the edge of the chair that's off to the side of the piano. "Then they'll want you to audition for the donor. It's up to the donor to decide who gets to use the violin."

I sit down on the piano bench and cross my arms.

"What's wrong?"

"No offense, Miss Sinclair, but how can I audition on your old violin?"

"You won't be using that one. You'll use this instead." She points to her rare violin sitting on the shelf across the room.

"Seriously?" I look right at her and when I open my mouth to talk, I'm choked up and simply say, "Thank you."

"It's a bit tricky, though." She scoots back into the seat and crosses her left leg over her right.

"Would it be okay with you if I come over to practice on it?" I unzip my backpack and get out my sheet music for my lesson.

"That's not what I meant by tricky, Cassie." She gets up and moves the music stand so it's aligned with the mirror. "What I mean is that we have to try and avoid the *reason* you need a new violin."

"Can't we just say I need to play on a really good instrument?" I stand up. "It's the truth."

"We can." She points to my music, which I hand to her, and she sets it on the music stand. "But you may be asked about your . . . previous violin's history. That conversation might wander to places where we really don't want it to go." She smoothes the sheet flat against the stand.

"Oh." My excitement dissolves and I sit back down, not knowing what to say.

She turns around and clasps her hands. "We can't lie about what happened to your violin. But if the benefactor knows the truth, she isn't likely to lend you such a valuable violin."

"I see your point."

"So before that happens, we need to try and steer clear of your broken Mangenot"—she gets her violin case from the shelf, lays it on the chair, and opens it—"at all costs."

I sigh.

"Let's not worry about it right now, okay?" She hands me her violin. "Let's just get to work." She smiles at me.

Her violin feels awkward under my chin. I search for a comfortable position, and when I play a few scales, my forearms are still tender from batting. Moving, gliding, the ache smoothes out and I begin the Tchaikovsky.

Miss Sinclair stands beside me, tapping her foot for the tempo. "You're rushing the triplet."

I stop playing.

"Try it again."

I do, and when I'm through, she simply says, "Good."

I continue until I get to a difficult passage.

"Your bow is coming off the string too much."

I stop.

"Remember to connect."

I make a note to myself, marking the passage.

When I try it again, she sings me through it. I move from being out there all alone, to aligning myself with her. After a while, she says, "Your G's out of tune."

I stop to tune it.

When I start up again, she continues to sing. I hear her tone and work to match it perfectly. "Crescendo!" she shouts. In and out of the notes I move. "Spiccato," she says, "but don't make it choppy." When I'm done, she says, "Good. That was *very* good." I play on, listening, trying to get my positioning right. I think of Nick at the batting cage, telling me to trust my hands. That's what I'm doing now. I'm focusing on my hands, on having faith in them to do what I need them to do.

When I finish, Miss Sinclair tells me to sit on the bench. She sits in the chair beside me. "How are things with your dad?"

"He and Mom call each other every night." I rest the violin in my lap, still holding the bow. "She had dinner with him last week."

"What about you? Have you talked with him?"

"No, not yet." The words come out quietly.

She turns toward me and leans closer. "You haven't spoken to him since you got back?"

I look at her, and after a few seconds I decide to tell her the truth. "No. I've been too scared."

She reaches for the violin, then takes the bow from me. "It's time, Cassie. It's time to move past what happened."

"I know."

She puts the violin and bow back into the case. "The longer you avoid him, the longer you're putting off your own healing, and the harder it'll get." She latches the case and the loud click echoes.

"I should get going now." I stand up. "I'm actually meeting him in a little while."

"Tonight?" She stands.

"Yes. At his hotel. I'm meeting him in the lobby."

"Is your mom going with you?"

"No. I want to see him alone."

"And she's okay with this?"

"Yes—we talked about it. We'll be in a public place. He's on medication—and he's a lot calmer, according to my mom."

"Good luck, my dear." She pats me gently on the shoulder.

I quickly put on my winter layers to go outside. After I say goodbye, I don't hear Miss Sinclair close the door behind me like she usually does. I turn around and she's standing there, watching me go. I wave and she waves back. Then I head down the steps and out into the cold.

49

We're in the lobby of the hotel and we're just standing there, looking at each other. Dad's lost weight. He's acting like he's been a bad boy and I'm his mother, coming to talk about his punishment. It makes me feel weird to see him so unsure of himself. I step back when he moves toward me, hoping he isn't going to hug me. He doesn't. Instead, he points to the grouping of chairs in front of the fireplace and sits down after me.

Neither of us says anything for a while. But when he faces me, I notice the scar above his left cheek. It's always been part of his face, but now I wonder if Grandpa hit him years ago. His brown eyes begin to soften and I take off my jacket. The fire catches my attention when it crackles. I like how it warms my feet.

"Cassie, are you okay?"

"I think so."

"Look, I have a lot to say. But first I need to ask you something."

"What's that?"

"Well, I know you went to Pretoria—to see your grandfather. He didn't hurt you, did he?"

"No, he just sort of yelled at me, and then he ignored me. Finally I decided to leave. He didn't even care that I was alone, with no way to get home."

Dad shakes his head, looking regretful.

"How could he be so mean to me? It was almost dark. I had no money. How could he just let me leave to try and figure it out for myself, a girl all alone in a strange neighborhood?"

"That's how he is. He used to pull shit like that with me all the time."

"What do you mean?"

"Sometimes he just snaps. He'd do this thing where sometimes he wouldn't show up to give me a ride home after orchestra practice. We had rehearsals a long way from our house, too."

"He did that a lot?"

"Yes. And he'd never apologize. Instead, he'd give me the same old excuse—he wanted 'to build my character.' Yeah, *right*. All it did was piss me off."

I suddenly feel sick to my stomach—like I might puke.

"Of course, his folks built his character doing the same kinds of things. When he was your age, they sold his violin."

"What are you talking about?"

"They were poor. He'd been awarded a rare violin and a scholarship to study at a conservatory. But they needed the money—they wanted to emigrate from Prague. While he was at school, they took his violin to a dealer. Sold it without him even knowing about it. He came home and found out his whole future had changed."

I'm stunned. I've never heard this part of my family's story before. It almost sounds too strange to be true. But with everything that's happened lately, it sure *feels* true. And that's when another weird thing happens—Winnie's dad walks into the lobby. I sink down into my chair, hoping he won't notice us, but Dad calls to him, "Bob?"

Mr. Williams stops and zeroes in on me, like I'm sitting by myself.

"Is something wrong?" Dad asks him.

He shakes his head. "Does your mom know you're here, Cassie?"

"Yes. It's okay, Mr. Williams."

"Oh. Okay. Well, uh, actually Frank, I came to speak with you, but I can come back later." He starts to leave, then turns around and says to Dad, "You know, I'll just take a minute here, if you don't mind."

"Have a seat," Dad points to the vacant chair next to him. By the look on his face, I can tell he's not in the mood to talk to him, but he's pushing himself to be different— patient and polite.

"Frank, I heard what happened—you know—to Cassie's violin. I just want to ask you to consider getting help with—uh—your situation."

"It's nice of you to care, Bob, but it's not really any of your business."

"Actually, Frank, it is. Cassie and Winnie are best friends and Cass is like a daughter to me and Alice. And my daughter is at your house all the time. I don't want her to have to deal with any kind of upsetting episodes like that one."

211

"Oh. Okay, I see."

When Dad doesn't go on, Mr. Williams says, "I could get you a referral. My brother's a social worker."

After more silence, Dad finally speaks. "I've already been seeing a therapist."

"Glad to hear it, Frank. I want Cassie to be okay. You've hurt her a great deal. The harder you try, the easier it'll be for her to get her life back on track. And for her to ever trust you again."

I begin to tear up so I look away. It feels good knowing that Winnie's dad cares about me this much, that he'd talk to my dad like this. And it's sad that he even needs to say those words.

"She's a great kid and an awesome violinist. She deserves to have a father who's in her court."

"I'm trying," Dad says, choking up.

"Good. I'm glad to hear it. That's all I have to say. Thanks for hearing me out." He stands up and reaches out to shake Dad's hand.

Dad stands up, hesitates, and then nods his head as he shakes Mr. Williams's hand.

"I'll see you soon, Cassie," he says, smiling at me.

"Okay."

After he leaves, Dad leans back, exhales, and stares at the ceiling.

I sigh. Watching several people meander toward the front desk to check in, my mind returns to what Dad just told me about my grandfather. I struggle with confusing images of Grandpa that shift like clouds changing shape. I try to understand that the sweet old man who gave me the

Mangenot is the same person who didn't care about me after I told him it was gone. Now I find out he was mean to my dad *on purpose*. And that *his* parents treated him horribly, too.

And I can so *totally* relate to what it must've felt like—the rage—at having your parents sell your violin. But I can't relate to turning around and being so mean to your own son, and your granddaughter, too. Over time, Grandpa went from good to bad, bad to good, and then bad to worse. And Dad's changing, too. Maybe from bad to better. I hope so, but who knows?

Dad interrupts my thoughts. "Cassie, I need to ask you a favor. I'd really appreciate it if you'd come to one of my therapy sessions. You don't have to answer tonight, but I could really use some help from my psychiatrist in talking through some things with you, Mom, and Michael."

I look at him and wonder if he has any more interesting family secrets to tell me about. And since I'm not sure I'm up for any more surprises, I don't commit myself to going. "I'll think about it, okay?"

"Fair enough." He stands up. "We should get going. I promised your mother I'd get you home in time to practice tonight."

We walk to the car in silence, and even after we get in, neither of us says anything all the way to the house.

Mom's watching for me and I see her at the window as Dad pulls up. When I'm on the steps she opens the door and waves to Dad. I'm not even in the house yet and she's hugging me tight, almost the way Winnie's parents hug me sometimes. When she finally lets go, she has tears in her eyes. "I know it must've been really hard to face him." She looks directly into my eyes and says, "I'm so proud of you."

I'm still stuck at the part where Grandpa's parents sold his violin, so I'm not ready to talk to her yet. When I have my coat off, she takes my hand, saying, "C'mon, I'll make us some cocoa." I follow her but I don't help. Instead I plop down into the chair and rest my head on the table. I hear her busily clattering pans. She opens the fridge, turns on the stove. Her noisy energy makes me realize how tired I am.

Mom sets down two steaming mugs and sits at the table. It's the good cocoa—not instant stuff—it's the real kind, made with milk and three kinds of chocolate. It's almost too sweet when I sip at it. I burn my lip.

I push it away and get up from my chair. "Mom, I have to go to bed. I'm totally wiped out."

"Okay, Cassie, go get some rest." She gets up and hugs me again, even longer this time. "It's going to get better." She moves the stray strands of hair off my face. "I promise."

50

Red slashes mark the days on the calendar taped beside my computer monitor. Winnie picks it up to get a closer look. "What's this?"

"Nick and me—we're marking down the days until his visit."

"You're really into him."

"Only twenty-six more days until I see him again."

"Don't go all dreamy on me now." She points at my violin case. "You have work to do."

"Geez, Win. You're worse than the conductor." I sit down at my desk.

"Do you want a new violin or not, Cass?"

She's right. I've asked her to come over and help me get ready for my audition. Even though she doesn't play the violin, she's really picky and her feedback makes me play better.

I start playing scales: A, D, then G, and then some warm-ups. Finally I start in on Tchaikovsky, and this is what happens: I play, she stops me. I try her suggestion, she stops me. I try it again, she smiles. I continue, she stops me.

We go on like this for almost an hour. Then, when I get to the cadenza, we have a long discussion. I try to play it three times but I still can't get it.

"I think we need goddess intervention," Winnie says. She lights a few candles. She stands before me and taps my head. "Now close your eyes."

I want to scream at her to just let me try it again, but I don't. Instead I shut my eyes and keep quiet.

She places her hand on my head like she's blessing me. "Oh feminine face of God, I call to you. Violin Girl needs your help. Please send her guidance."

I open my eyes.

"Let's call it quits for today, Cassie."

"I can't, Win." I smooth out the sheet music. "My audition's only three days away!"

"Then take a little break. You're pushing way too hard and it never comes when you pressure yourself like that."

"You're right." I put the violin away and flop back on my bed.

Win sits at my computer. "You're really stressed out about this audition, Cass," she says as she checks her email on my computer. "You weren't even this bad for your solo at the fall concert."

"But Win, I might not get it—even if I'm great." I curl into a ball.

She taps at the keyboard. "There's that much competition for this instrument?"

"No, that's not it. It's worse than that. If they find out Dad broke my Mangenot, I'll never get it, no matter what."

"But *you* didn't break it," she says between mouse

clicks, then she looks up. "Besides, he doesn't live here anymore!"

I sit up. "I don't think they care about that. They'll see it as too much of a risk for such a rare, valuable instrument."

"What did Miss Sinclair say about it?"

"She told me to avoid the topic."

"How would they even find out what happened?"

"They might ask me—you know, stuff like how long I've been playing, what kind of violin I've been using, and why I need this one. All those things could come up."

"So what are you going to say?"

"I don't know yet, Win."

She turns back around to face the screen. "Don't think about it for now." She signs off and says, "Just focus on playing your best."

"Yeah, I guess." I stand up and take Calliope off my printer. "But I really want and need a new violin." I sit on the end of my bed and cradle Calliope.

Winnie sits down beside me and pets Calliope's belly. "Can't your mom get you a new one?"

"She wants to, but it costs a fortune. Plus, it's complicated. Because of Dad." I reposition Calliope on my lap. "Your dad talked to him."

Winnie looks at me wide-eyed.

"He told you, right?"

"Yeah. You know my dad, Cass—he's an old hippie— all about 'Peace, love the earth and all God's children.' You're like another one of his kids."

"I know."

"The night we sat parked in front of your house looking for Calliope, he told me the only way he could see things working out for you—as a family and with the violin—is if your dad went into therapy."

"Wow." I gently rub Calliope's ears. "He's amazing—the way he's trying so hard to help me."

"Yeah. He's one of a kind, I guess."

Calliope closes her eyes like she's in bliss. "But I've been thinking about something else."

"What? Nick?" she asks with a mischievous grin.

I poke her with my elbow and Calliope opens her eyes. "Come on, Win. There's room in my brain for more than just Nick and the violin."

"Well, you sure had me fooled." Now she's giggling.

"Seriously, Win. Listen. I want to do a benefit concert."

"Wow. I wasn't expecting you to say that. Where'd that come from, anyway?"

Calliope moves around, then finds a comfortable spot in my lap. "I want to do a benefit concert for the homeless. And I'm really serious about this. "

"Awesome!" She sits cross-legged on my bed. "I'll help you with it."

"I want to donate the proceeds to Hannah's House."

Winnie picks up Calliope and puts her in her lap. "That could work." She smiles as she strokes the cat's smooth hair.

I get up and pick up my violin. "Do you think we could have it at your church?"

"That's a great idea. They have all kinds of concerts there."

I begin Lalo's Symphony Espanol. "You know, Win, I

always wanted to perform at Unity Temple." I play on, envisioning myself standing at the front of the sanctuary, performing to a full house. I can picture myself looking out, seeing the people—imagining them in the pews—each one filling up. They'll be the kind of audience to make donations that'll put fast-food gift cards into the pockets of a lot of homeless girls.

We walk toward Dad's psychiatrist's office and my heart is pounding a mile a minute, and rattling in between beats. And I feel like I'm going to throw up. At the door, the psychiatrist, Lydia—who appears to be a little older than Mom—introduces herself to Mom, Michael, and me like we're at a dinner party. I wish we were. I'd rather be just about anywhere else than here.

Chairs are set up in a circle and Dad's sitting there alone, waiting. He's not hyper—just a little bit nervous. Mom takes the nearest seat beside him and Michael sits on his other side. I sit across from Dad. After closing the door, Lydia sits between Mom and me.

I look around the room. It's pleasant and I bet when the sun hits the Monet print during the day, the flowers come alive. Dad looks down at the floor. Mom's sitting straight and proper in her navy business suit, like she's expecting to get an A because we look nice. Except Michael doesn't look nice. His clothes are all wrinkled and he's tired from hours on the bus from Cleveland after a week of finals.

With his outstretched legs—ankles crossed—and his arms folded tight across his chest, he looks like I feel: defensive and kind of wiped out. I'm totally jealous of Winnie, because I'm sure she'll never get summoned to family therapy.

We sit quietly like this for what seems like hours and I wonder why Lydia doesn't say something already. Finally, Dad says, "Thanks for coming."

"We need help, Frank," Mom says.

"Why don't we talk about why we're here?" Lydia says.

I look over at Dad, who's staring at the floor. Wisps of thoughts pass through my mind, but they're too fast for me to process. I want to talk about my broken violin, but it feels too risky. *Calm Dad could easily switch back into Angry Dad*, I think to myself. I immediately see my violin crashing—it's still vivid and fresh—while my triumphant debut as a soloist feels more like some other lifetime.

"Dad—," I say. But I stop, take a deep breath, and exhale. I rub my arms. *Be strong like the violin goddess*, I tell myself. "You haven't been the same since I started practicing to be a soloist." I'm not sure he's hearing me, but it's important so I push ahead anyway. "I know that you broke your own violin when you were my age."

"What?" Michael asks.

"So the old man told you about that?" Dad's face is now turning red and his right knee is bouncing up and down. I can feel the tension rising, filling in the space between us.

"He did, but he didn't tell me why." I'm tapping my

feet on the floor in quick-time. "All I know is that you guys had a fight."

Red blotches are showing up on Dad's neck, and his upper lip is sweaty. "It was a long time ago, okay?" Dad says.

"Yes, it was, Frank," says Lydia, "but with PTSD, old wounds cause suffering until they're healed. The way to heal this is to talk about it."

"PTSD?" Michael asks. "Like what some of the Iraq vets have?"

"Yes, but let's focus on what happened between your dad and his dad, first," says Lydia. "And then we'll talk a lot more about your question, okay, Michael?"

Michael nods.

"What happened—I mean, why did you break your violin?" I ask.

Dad blows air out his mouth, sits up, does a neck roll. "I broke my violin," he shifts so that he's looking at me, "to stop my old man from having a reason to beat the shit out of me anymore."

The news jolts me in the chest.

Mom gasps.

Dad's neck is more blotchy than before. I'm afraid he's about to explode, fueled with rage just thinking about my grandfather. "I was never good enough for him," he says, looking out the window, sounding almost like a child.

I'm barely breathing, feeling a chill even though my armpits seem to be taking a shower.

"He was always on me to practice." Dad pauses. He

looks like he's left the room, on a journey back into the past. "He even locked me up sometimes."

"What do you mean?" Mom asks, as I curl up into my-self so I fit like a tight ball in the chair.

"When I was Cassie's age, he used to lock me in my room for hours. . . ."

"Go on Frank," says Lydia. I wonder if she's forcing herself to say what she's supposed to say, but isn't really sure she wants to hear the rest.

"To make sure I practiced."

Shock fills me up and every muscle in my body goes tense.

"I thought he'd be satisfied when I became concert-master, but that only made him push me into the concerto competition—to play a solo with the orchestra."

"So you won and became a soloist?" Mom asks.

"Yes."

I'm clutching myself, holding on tight because it feels like the ceiling is about to fall. Still, I force myself to get the answers I need.

"So what happened?" I ask.

Dad puts his head in his hands. He starts to weep, and then goes into full throttle sobbing.

Lydia reaches behind her, snatches the box of tissues off her desk, and hands it to Dad. Mom puts her arm around him, but he doesn't accept her comfort.

I wait a bit, then say, "It's okay, Dad."

He looks up then and blows his nose. "You know the Prokofiev Concerto?"

"Yes. Sure."

"Well, I knew it very well," he says, staring out the window. "But when it was time to go on stage, I started shaking. The room began to spin, and I felt like I was going to puke. I even started getting chest pains—I thought I was having a heart attack."

"Oh no!" I exclaim. I remember when this happened last year to Ariel. "Was it stage fright?"

Dad nods. "But I didn't know that at the time," he says. "And I never even made it to the stage."

It's a musician's worst nightmare—and it's hard to imagine him going through it.

"My old man beat the shit out of me that night."

"He beat you up for having stage fright?" I ask.

Dad nods. "Said I humiliated the whole family." He leans back, exhales, and stares at the ceiling with tears still on his cheeks. "And that's when *I* snapped. I wanted it to be over. So I threw that violin against the wall as hard as I could."

I sigh and look at the ceiling, too. *My Mangenot.* "So basically, my playing was bringing back all these bad memories for you?"

"Yes," Dad whispers.

We both should go to the ER for broken hearts, except when I finally look in his direction, I see him gazing at me. Somehow he's still in one piece, sort of. And amazingly, so am I.

52

Dad passes the box of tissues to Mom, who takes one and dabs it at each eye. For a while, no one says anything, which is good because I'm trying to absorb these new family secrets. Michael and I look at each other, and though we haven't exchanged words, I get it that we're both glad we're not alone with all of this.

"Frank, I know it was really hard," Lydia says, "but I'm glad you could tell them about your father—especially about this terrible fight the two of you had."

He nods.

"It's an important step toward healing this pain you've been living with for such a long time."

"Yeah, Dad—I'm really sorry to hear this happened to you," Michael says, "and I'll do whatever it takes to help you to feel better."

"Frank," Mom says, "I love you and I really need you to be stable."

He looks at her and he's about the saddest I've ever seen him.

"I need you to manage your anger," she says. "You

can't take out your problems on vases and violins, let alone on me, Cassie, Michael, or the cat."

"I'm trying, Jeannine," he whispers.

"Today is a really good start, Frank," Lydia says.

Mom says, "For us to even consider living together again as a family—to have you come home—the violence has to stop."

"I know that, Jeannine."

"It's important for her to say it, Frank," says Lydia. "For herself, and for Cassie's sake."

"And," Mom says, "I can't ever take the chance that you'll put our daughter in jeopardy or make her feel like she has to run away to be safe. Our home must be safe. For people and for cats. It can never happen again. Otherwise, no matter how much I love you, I'll divorce you."

"C'mon, I feel like I'm getting beat up here."

"Frank," says Lydia, "this is different from what you experienced as a child. This is someone who truly loves you and what she's asking for is good for both of you."

Dad begins to cry again.

"I thought you had an anxiety disorder," says Michael. "That's why I was confused when Lydia said PTSD."

"Anxiety can sometimes be a signal that there are deeper issues," Lydia says. "I suggested medication for your dad, so that he could feel more comfortable, more in control, and to support him as he talks about what happened to him as a child."

I look across at Dad and he seems calmer.

"So is it like what soldiers get?" Michael asks.

"Some of them," Lydia says. "Similar symptoms, but

different trauma. Your dad has agreed to talk with me about growing up with your grandfather. If he can put these traumas to rest, he may or may not still need the meds. In the meantime, they're helping him control his temper."

I watch Dad as he quietly listens to Lydia and Michael talk. Then he leans forward and says, "I just need to say something here."

"What is it, Frank?" Lydia asks.

Through tears, Dad turns to me and chokes out, "What your mom is asking of me, Cassie—I—I know—it's what's best for all of us. And I'll try my best to make it happen. That's why I came to see Lydia."

"But we don't have to hear all the details, do we?" I ask, nervously.

"Not unless you want to know more and your dad is comfortable telling you," Lydia answers.

"Now I get it," I say. "It was so confusing before—I mean, I didn't get why my playing the violin, and especially why being a soloist, was making you act so crazy and getting you so upset."

"Well. Now you know," Dad says. "I wish it didn't affect me this way, but it did. I never meant to hurt anyone, especially not you, Cassie."

"It's a trigger," Lydia says. "Your becoming a soloist, Cassie, triggered bad, traumatic memories, and that's why your dad got so upset. What happened in the past affected his behavior in the present. For your dad, it's just as if the traumas from his teen years were happening all over again, right now."

"I'm sorry, Dad," I say. "I'm really sorry that my playing brought up such bad memories."

"No, you don't have to apologize," Dad says. "I'm the one who's sorry." He looks at me, then at Michael, and finally at Mom. "It's not your problem or your fault. It's *my* problem and I have to find a way to cope with it."

"What I'd like to know is—Mom, why'd you ever get me started with the violin in the first place? I mean, why not the flute? Or a sport, like soccer?"

Mom smiles. "When Michael was just a baby, I read an article on parenting that explained how music supports the learning process. I wanted to give you and Michael the advantage, a one-up on everyone else." She points at Michael. "But you were having none of it. You played tennis with your dad and those were the only lessons you were interested in."

"I remember." Michael nods.

"But Cassie—you liked the idea. Your dad played violin as a kid—and Frank, I thought you'd get a kick out of having a child who played. I never expected it to cause so much trouble for you."

Dad sighs.

"When I first mentioned the idea to you, Cassie, you seemed to already *be* a violinist."

I smile at her. When I shift to make eye contact with Dad, he nods encouragingly at me.

"I guess you know I'm not giving it up," I tell Dad.

"You shouldn't have to change what you do—you shouldn't miss out on playing the violin because of me. And I don't want you to. I never wanted that, Cass."

"You don't?"

"No. You love it. And you're so gifted. So much more than I ever would have been."

Now it's my turn to cry, and Mom passes me the box of tissues.

Lydia pats my shoulder. "We're just about out of time, but I want to give you all an assignment."

"Please . . . ," Michael says, "I just finished finals."

Lydia smiles. "In the next week, I want you to go out for a family dinner. Do something normal. Something to reinforce the great work you've done here today."

Dad smiles at her.

Lydia looks at me. "Do you think you can handle that?"

"I think so," I say. Although I don't admit to her that I'm not sure I'll be ready so soon—during this next week—to deal with a family dinner that includes Dad.

"Sounds good," Mom says.

"As long as I don't have to cram for it," Michael says, "I think I can handle it."

I'm dreaming again:

I'm three years old. I'm wearing a soft nightgown with billowy sleeves, trimmed with ribbons. My hair is woven with matching ribbons and it all flows down my back.

On the coffee table is a cereal box with loopy red lettering. When I pick it up I see it looks like a musical instrument. It has a neck made from an old paint stirrer. Purple yarn blooms out of the front, attaching at the bottom like strings. There's a dowel-rod bow beside it.

I place my cereal box violin under my chin, and when I position the bow, I play Mozart Adagio in E major for Violin and Orchestra. I dance all around, in and out of the furniture, all around the room. A baby violin goddess playing, playing, playing.

Then it's dark, except for a spotlight, following me wherever I go. My movement transforms from walking to stepping into the air, to drifting, like a brilliant butterfly, buoyant in space, fluttering, and flashing. I'm flying.

We decide to do our family counseling assignment, even though Michael's visiting Melanie in Ohio and can't join us. Mom and Dad want to keep the positive momentum going, so they talked me into having dinner together tonight.

Mom gets off early from work and we meet Dad at our favorite Chinese restaurant. We haven't been here in a really long time, but nothing in the place has changed. We take a booth next to a window that looks into the kitchen. I slide in first, like always, so I can get the best view of the chefs as they work. Mom slides in beside me, and we're both across from Dad.

After we order, Dad looks at me and asks, "How are you, Cassie?"

"I can't stop thinking about everything," I say, looking over at him. "You know, about you and Grandpa."

"Oh? Is there more you need or want to talk about?" He sounds a bit jittery.

Flames rise up and catch my attention as they heat up an enormous wok. "I was shocked about what you told me at Lydia's." I take a sip of water. "Now it seems like a heavy weight, and something really bad—and complicated—that happened to you."

Mom nods.

Dad looks at Mom. "I'm just beginning to deal with it now, after half a lifetime."

I start to say something, but I let out a breath instead.

Dad looks at me. "What were you going to say, Cass? It's okay to tell me."

I decide to just go for it. "When I was getting ready for my solo, I just wish it would've brought up happy memories for you—instead of these horrible ones."

He's not looking dazed anymore. It's more like he's here, right here, with me, and he's not angry. Just nervous. "Yeah, me, too." He grips the edge of the table. "Having my old man show up for your concert was too much for me that night. It sent me right over the edge." The sadness and guilt linger in his voice. "I didn't even know how much I'd stored up inside me. I never expected to get so out of control."

"Frank, I'm really sorry. I just didn't know," Mom says. "I'd never have invited him if I'd had the slightest idea about what he did to you."

"I know that you meant well," Dad says. "That you were trying to do something good, both for Cassie and for my old man."

"And for you," Mom says. "I'd hoped the concert would start to bring you two back together."

The waitress arrives with our appetizers and we all eat for a while.

When he's done, Dad pushes away his bowl and plate, then he speaks: "I didn't want either of you to know any-thing—about my past. But now that you do, I'm actually starting to feel better. I guess it wasn't good to keep it all bottled up." His words come out all shaky, like his voice is on stilts.

"I'm glad it's helping." Mom tears up again, and reaches in her purse for a tissue. "I just wish you could've told me—so you didn't have to suffer alone like that all this time."

The waitress brings the steaming dishes of our main course and we dig in. Now Mom and Dad chat about work and normal things, but I don't say anything. Eating has never been the same for me, ever since my night at the shel-ter. Before I was there, I just took food for granted and never even gave it a thought. Now I make sure to taste and appreciate every flavor and notice all the textures. I savor the crunchy cashews—they're exactly why I love this dish so much.

After a while, Dad says, "I think—I'm not sure, but I think there's hope for us." His eyes are watery but he doesn't actually cry.

I keep quiet and sip my water.

"There is if we work at it," Mom says, looking into his eyes.

Dad reaches for my hand. "Cassie, I'm so sorry about what I did to you. For all of it."

Now I begin to cry. The doors that were closed over my heart spring open. I'm surprised that I want to forgive him, and now I'm crying even harder. These tears are be-cause I want my family back.

Mom puts her arm around me and Dad hands me his handkerchief. We sit there in silence, each lost in our own thoughts, until the waitress brings a tray of orange wedges and fortune cookies.

Dad holds out the tray for me. I take a fortune cookie, open it, and slip out the fortune inside. I read it to myself first, then out loud to my parents: "'Your love shines bright on another.'" They both nod, solemnly, as if this were the most profound message ever found in a fortune cookie.

Then Dad smiles at me and says, "Did we ever tell you why we named you Cassandra?"

"No."

He smiles at Mom, then tells me, "Because it means 'inspiring love.'"

"Fitting, don't you think?" Mom asks Dad.

"Definitely," he says, looking straight into my eyes. Then he grabs a cookie, gently cracking it open. "'Listen and you will make great strides.'" He smiles, then waves the fortune. "That's really good advice, especially right now."

Mom's says: "'Friendship is a rose worth its thorns.'" Her whole face relaxes. "Yes. And roses *are* my favorite flower." She says this looking into Dad's eyes.

Now I have to look away because it's kind of embarrassing. I sort of feel out of place, almost like I'm along on my parents' date.

Then we talk for a while, almost like nothing important has come up during this dinner. Dad asks me about school, then about Winnie and Nick. Finally he asks, "How are things going with Miss Sinclair?" and I pause. I can tell that something's happened—he's changing; he's different, more open. It's sort of nice. I answer, saying, "It's rough—I'm working on Tchaikovsky—I can't seem to get the cadenza."

Now the waitress hands him the check. He pays for dinner and I wonder if Mom's going to lose it since we're not all going home together. But she stays calm and keeps it together. "I'll call you later, Frank," she says, looking straight into his eyes.

He nods, and with a sad smile puts his billfold away.

Mom slides out of the booth, and I start to get up. But then Dad surprises me: "Did your mom tell you I bought the CD of the Tchaikovsky piece?"

"You did?"

"Yes." He nods.

I do a double take—to be sure this guy is my actual dad.

"With that cadenza," he goes on, "the point is to give it energy while you reach for depth."

I sit there, thinking about what he's saying. Then I smile. Because it makes sense. If I approach it that way, I can tell that it'll be right. "Thanks, Dad," I say, amazed and glad at the same time. "That helps."

"No problem, Cassie. I'm sure you're going to nail it."

Once we're in Mom's car I wave goodbye to him, and we drive off.

"That worked out okay for you, Cass, I mean our family dinner assignment?" she asks.

"Yes. I think we actually aced it."

A few days later, we arrive for my audition at the bene-factor's house. An older woman opens the door—and she's someone who instantly makes me wish she were my grand-mother. Dressed in a silk pantsuit and wearing a medallion, her flat shoes look like ballet slippers. Her gray hair is per-fectly coifed, and she's very elegant. "Hello. I assume you're Eva Sinclair?" she asks.

"Hello, Mrs. Bern. It's very good to meet you. Thank you for seeing us."

"I'm delighted to meet you, too. Please come in."

We step inside the foyer, and after they shake hands, Miss Sinclair says, "And this is Cassandra Prochazka."

We shake hands. "Hello, Mrs. Bern."

"Please, dear. Call me Amelia."

I nod and smile my thanks for this, and feel a bit less nervous.

"Cassandra, I see you've brought your bow," she says.

I nod. Then we follow her down a long hallway through her elegant home. Each room we pass appears to be specially decorated. I wish Mom could see it. She'd love this house.

"It would be proper for us to sit in the living room," she says, pointing to it as we pass it. "But I prefer my sunroom. It's so much brighter and more comfortable." When we arrive there, she invites us to sit.

Now I see why she prefers this room. It's casual compared to the living room, and it's full of wicker furniture with overstuffed cushions. Accent pillows are everywhere and a vase of fresh roses sits on an end table. Bookcases crammed with every type of volume line the wall opposite a lit fireplace that crackles. Tall, sheer curtained French doors open out to a terrace.

I sit at the far end of the sofa by the fireplace; Miss Sinclair takes a nearby chair. A tea set and plates with tiny sandwiches and fancy cookies wait on the glass coffee table in front of the sofa. I want to lean back and settle into the soft comfortable pillows, but I'm trying to look grown-up, responsible and trustworthy, so I sit up straight on the edge of my chair.

Amelia sits on the sofa beside me and pours us each a cup of tea. "Help yourself to the goodies, dear," she says.

I take a bite of a leaf-shaped cookie with chocolate frosting and try to be dainty while sipping my tea.

"Well," Amelia says, "I know you didn't come here for a tea party."

"No," Miss Sinclair smiles, "but it's lovely just the same. Thank you for your hospitality."

"Not at all. But I was young once," she says, smiling at me, "and tea parties bored me to death back then."

I smile at her, liking her even more.

"If I were you, Cassandra, I'd want to get my audition over with so I could relax."

"We're not in a hurry, Amelia. There's no rush," says Miss Sinclair.

I echo her to be polite.

"Don't be silly, dear," she says, standing up. "It'll only take me but a minute to get the violin for you."

I remember, then, what Miss Sinclair's told me about Amelia's violin. It was built in 1735 and it's worth a million dollars. I cross my left leg over my right, then uncross it again. I fidget nervously, shifting in my seat. Then I sit up straight and cross my right leg over my left, worrying about what's coming.

Miss Sinclair presses firmly on my knee, "Cassie, relax," she says. "It's going to be fine."

I take a deep breath and exhale slowly. As I let out my breath, Amelia returns carrying a new violin case. She places it before me on the coffee table. I run my hand over the case.

"Open it!" Amelia says as she sits down.

I open the latch and lift the lid. It's lined in purple velvet.

Miss Sinclair gasps. "What a beautiful Carlo Bergonzi!"

Amelia nods to me, and I carefully take out the violin. Even though it's very old, it feels very sturdy. The varnish glows thickly over the wood's grain, making it look like strands of fine shiny hair blended with shades of red and chestnut. I run my fingers over the strings. It's like I'm touching silk.

"It's a beauty," Amelia says. "It makes me wish I were young and just beginning. Then I'd play in the youth symphony, too."

"Do you play?" asks Miss Sinclair.

"Oh no, but I'm mad about the violin. I've had season tickets to the symphony for decades."

Miss Sinclair gets up and takes the case from me, then sits back down. "Let's get started," she says.

I stand, and as a warm-up, I play my solo for a few minutes. The hem of my dress dances around my ankles as I move. When I feel calm enough and ready, I begin playing Tchaikovsky. Steadily, I step into his notes, playing them, interpreting them, feeling their power. The music paints a picture of butterflies in flight. I settle in, breathing the music—feel it washing over me like waves. I play on and listen, feeling myself become someone new.

Amelia stands up when I finish. Then she kisses me on the cheek and says, "You're the one."

"Thank you," I start to say, but the words come out choked by tears.

Amelia—who only comes up to my nose—puts both her hands on my shoulders: "I like the way you play, Cassandra. You've got guts."

I can feel my face flushing as I look at Miss Sinclair.

We sit down again and I carefully hold the violin in my lap.

"What kind of violin have you been playing up till now?"

I stiffen, then look at Miss Sinclair, who's acting like this is nothing unusual. "A Mangenot."

"Very nice." She smiles at me. "Will you be passing it on?"

I look down at the exquisite violin in my lap. "Uh, no."

She turns to Miss Sinclair, saying, "That's a shame."

I fidget in my seat, staring at the floor.

"Why aren't you passing it on?"

When Miss Sinclair doesn't answer, I realize Amelia's talking to me.

"Uh—it's broken," I answer.

"Beyond repair?"

"Yes."

Somewhat startled, she looks at Miss Sinclair, searching for an explanation.

Miss Sinclair says nothing. She sits still, like she's waiting to pounce.

"Were you in an accident, dear?"

"No." I stop breathing. I feel myself shrinking, wanting to slip away through the curtains and out of the room through the French doors.

I look at her.

Amelia faces me.

I shift my gaze to Miss Sinclair, who's staring at her clasped hands. Maybe she's trying to work a magic spell to make this all go away.

Holding tight to the Carlo Bergonzi, I say, "My father wrecked it."

"I see," Amelia says. Then, turning to Miss Sinclair, she adds, "This is going to be a problem."

Miss Sinclair nods her head silently, sadly, in agreement.

"I'm going to have to reconsider, Cassandra." She takes the violin from me.

I release it, telling myself not to cry. I want to be strong, and I hold my head up. I look at Amelia and say, "I understand."

"Her father has since gone into therapy. He's being treated by a psychiatrist, Amelia," says Miss Sinclair. She folds and unfolds her hands. "And he's no longer living in the same house as Cassie."

"Hmm. I see. Well, I want to think about this situation for a while." She puts the violin in the case and latches it shut. "I'll call you in a few days, Eva."

Now I stand up. I say, "Thank you, Amelia."

She's cool, but polite. "You're welcome, Cassandra."

It's dark when we leave Amelia's, and the air is crisp and clear. There's a sliver of light shining on the stairs. We walk to Miss Sinclair's car in silence; it's all so disappointing, and I know she's upset. The whole thing feels confusing, as if we're walking through loud white noise.

Miss Sinclair starts the engine and turns the heat on high. Before she pulls out of the space, she looks at me and says, "I was hoping the Mangenot wouldn't come up, and when it did, that there was a better way to handle it."

Her words feel like a slap. I turn away and stare at the empty flower boxes under the windows on the house next to Amelia's. "I even thought about lying. It would've been easy enough. A lot easier than telling the truth," I say, returning her glance.

She doesn't say anything else, but turns her head and stares through the windshield.

"But I thought about it, and a goddess would tell the truth."

Air catches in her throat. Then she reaches over and touches my shoulder. The car finally feels warmer.

"I felt her—the violin goddess. While I was playing the Bergonzi. But I figured it out—she wasn't watching me from the sky, or guiding and lighting my way from some-where."

"What do you mean?"

"The goddess. She's inside me."

She nods. "Cassie, dear, she isn't just inside you. She *is* you."

"You think I'm a violin goddess?"

"Truly, I do. You—when you're making music on a violin—you're like a divine presence."

She leans over and hugs me. Then we sit there, smil-ing at each other. I don't know why I'm okay, because this night isn't turning out like I'd hoped. I was supposed to go home with a new violin. Instead, I'm going home empty-handed.

56

Miss Sinclair turns on the radio but then immediately turns it off. Listening to music doesn't feel right just now. Neither one of us says anything, and by the time we get back to Oak Park, I'm going back to being upset.

Stopping in front of my house, Miss Sinclair promises, "I'll call you as soon as I hear something."

"Please call me on my cell, okay?"

"Okay, dear. I will."

I move in slow motion and open the door.

"Pray, Cassie." She touches my back. "I will, too."

"Okay." I feel heavy, pulling myself out of her car. Then I say goodbye.

As soon as I step inside, Mom knows right away that something's wrong. She helps me take off my coat and follows me upstairs. I get into bed, clothes and all, and put my head beside Calliope's on my pillow. Mom sits at the end of the bed and Calliope sniffs my hair.

"Cassie, please tell me what happened tonight."

Exhausted, I tell her in excruciating detail how it felt playing the Bergonzi. I need her to know that I played my best ever, and then speed through the conversation with Amelia, trying not to feel her words as I repeat them to Mom. But the replay hurts too much.

"Did Eva fight for you?"

"Yes. She told Amelia about Dad—that he doesn't live here anymore. And that he's in therapy. But . . ."

"But what?"

"When we left, I got the feeling that Miss Sinclair wished I'd handled things differently about the Mangenot."

"What do you mean?"

"Like maybe I shouldn't have told the truth. But I told Miss Sinclair that I wanted to be honest."

"Cassie, sometimes we want to leave out parts of the truth because it can have serious repercussions. In this case, there's so much at stake, and Mrs. Bern doesn't know the entire story."

I lie there with my eyes closed, listening to her. "I know, Mom."

Then she pats my feet. "But I'm really glad you didn't lie to her."

I sit up. "But then why does it feel so bad?"

"Because you really wanted that violin, and it meant a lot to you." She hugs me now.

"She's going to think about it," I whisper into her shoulder.

"Don't give up yet, Cass." She pats my back. "She might just change her mind."

"I doubt it."

She lets go and looks into my eyes. "You still might get it, honey. Sometimes these things turn out differently than we expect."

"I can't talk anymore, Mom. I need to go to sleep, okay?"

Disappointment drags me down and pulls me into fitful sleep.

57

I somehow make it to school the next day. It's Tuesday and Winnie finds me just as I'm slamming my locker shut. She drags me down the hall, in the opposite direction of our first-period class.

"Where are we going?" I ask.

She pulls me into the restroom.

"We'll be late, Win."

"I don't care." She checks underneath all the stalls to make sure we're alone, then guides me to the last sink, in the corner. "I'm so sorry. I heard what happened."

"You know?" I lean on the sink.

"I called last night to see how it went but you'd already gone to bed. I talked to your mom." She puts her arm around my shoulder. The late bell rings and I automatically move toward the door. "Wait, Cass." She pulls me back. "Are you okay?"

"Actually, I'm numb."

"What happened?"

I tell her the whole, long, painful version. "Being without your very own instrument is like being without a country."

"Or like losing a body part," Win adds. She hugs me.

"You should've seen it—it's an actual Carlo Bergonzi."

"Wow." She steps back and looks at me.

"It killed me to have to hand it over, especially after she'd told me I was the one."

"I hope she chooses you again, Cass."

"It was bad enough when Dad broke the Mangenot. Then, when Miss Sinclair started talking about a benefactor . . . I got my hopes up. And now they're in the toilet. A person can't function without hope."

"Remember—goddess power."

I nod. But I can't feel it right now.

Then we get to class. Mr. Gold is so lost in the formula he's writing on the board that he doesn't even notice how late we are.

Between each class, I duck into the restroom and check for cell-phone messages. But there's nothing from Miss Sinclair. At lunch, when Tamika asks about my audition, I sound like a taped version of myself. "My audition went well. She wants to think about it. She'll tell me in a few days, and it's really hard to wait." If I tell the rest of the story I'll fall apart, so I keep it short. Then Winnie moves the conversation in another direction to get me off the hook.

I spot Dad's blue Jeep as I walk out of school with Winnie. When I get closer, he rolls down the passenger window. "Can I give you a lift?"

I look at Winnie, then back at Dad. "Okay."

Winnie turns me so my back is to Dad. "Are you sure, Cassie?"

"It's okay, Win." I turn back around to get in the car. "I'll call you later."

"Please do that." She waves at Dad as I climb in.

Dad waves back at her and, at the click of my seat belt, he pulls out into traffic.

"Don't you have to work today?"

"I got off early so we could talk." He turns toward our house. "Your mom called me last night and told me what happened." He slows to stop at the light. "You okay, Cassie?"

"Not really."

We drive on through town to our street. "I was thinking . . ."

I glance over at him. "What?"

"Maybe it would help if I called this benefactor."

"No, Dad. Don't."

"It's worth a try, Cass."

I think about my audition, and how it felt to play the Bergonzi. I remember the goddess guiding me. I say, "She's got enough information to make up her mind."

He doesn't argue with me. "If you change your mind, just call me, okay?" He pulls up in front of the house and we both sit there quietly. He looks longingly toward the bay window, as if he'd like to come home. But he just waits instead.

"Thanks for the ride." I open the door and hop out.

"Cassie."

I turn around to look at him. "Think it over. I'll do *any-thing* I can to help you. I mean it."

I try to smile, but tears flow instead. So I nod my head and slam the door. Inside, Calliope runs to the door to greet me. I drop my backpack, my coat, and everything else in a heap. Then I take my cell from my backpack, pick up Calliope, and carry her into the family room. There I lie down on the couch with my cat on my chest. Her purr is soothing, steady, and true.

When my cell rings it startles us both. I hold on to Calliope while I answer it, and I'm disappointed when it's not Miss Sinclair.

"What's wrong?" Nick says.

I'm too tired to go into much detail, so he gets the condensed version of the audition story.

"I'm really sorry to hear it, Cass." He sighs. "Are you okay?"

"I'm hanging in there, at least for the moment, anyway."

"She'll change her mind, Cass. You'll see."

"How do you know?" I ask.

"Because you deserve it, that's how."

"If only I'd fed Calliope that day. None of this would be happening."

"Cassie—stop blaming yourself. It's your dad's fault, not yours."

"I know that, Nick. But I just wish I could rewind that day and make it come out different."

"But then we wouldn't have met."

"You *know* I'm glad about that part, but who needs all this extra drama?"

"So rewind it, okay? Just don't edit out the part where we meet."

This is my first smile since the audition. But after we hang up, I still have to go back to waiting.

Waiting is hard.

I go through the motions and get through my classes. Walking around, I probably seem okay to everyone else. But inside, I'm like a total zombie. I'm a mess.

I try to make every day the same, just so that I know what's coming. I don't want any more surprises, and I want everything, hour to hour, to be a sure thing. For once I appreciate my boring school schedule. Five days a week, from eight to three, I know what's going to happen, and I know exactly what to expect. Even at lunch, since I'm the first one there, I always take the same table: the third one in along the wall.

I do the same thing at home, too. Each day I walk in, hold Calliope for a while, flip channels and watch nothing on TV. Then I practice: one- and two-finger scales up the fingerboard; shifting; three-octave scales; scales in double stops; and then bowing exercises. Then I move on to Lalo's Symphony Espanol. Then free play: I play whatever comes to mind, from phrases from my solo, to a scale, or bits and pieces from sonatas I've played in the past.

Then I eat dinner with Mom. Afterward, I hold Calliope some more. I do my homework. Nick calls me every night, still checking in with me. But I don't feel like talking much. So he tells me a joke, waits till I laugh, and then says, "I'll check in with you tomorrow." I go to bed with Calliope purring in my ear.

As the alarm rings each morning I repeat it all in the same order.

As the week wears on, no word from Amelia drains me. I feel like I've got a slow leak of energy and everything in my life feels flat to me. It's so bad that I haven't even crossed off the days till Nick's arrival, and I have no idea how many are left.

On Friday night, Michael returns from visiting his girlfriend. We don't talk about Amelia, and he's great about keeping me busy doing stuff with him. He's making sure I'm distracted.

Monday comes; I get through school and go to my lesson. There's no chitchat with Miss Sinclair. I walk in, set out the music, take up her violin, and I play—as if there isn't this giant question mark hanging in the air between us.

After three more days with no word, I wonder how much longer I can live in limbo.

Like I said, waiting is hard.

My cell rings and I stare at the number. I know it's Miss Sinclair's, but I'm too scared to answer it.

"Aren't you going to get that?" Michael asks. It's dinnertime on Friday night.

"Hello," I manage to say.

"Cassie? Can you be ready in half an hour?"

"Yes. What's going on?"

Mom and Michael stop eating and they're both staring at me.

"Amelia wants to see us."

"What about?"

"I think she's made a decision."

"Ohmigod. Okay, I'll be ready."

I hang up my cell and push my plate away. I tell Mom and Michael what's going on as I head up the stairs. I pick up a sleeping Calliope from her spot on my chair and hug her close. *Please Amelia, just say yes.* I set the cat down and yell downstairs. "Mom, I don't know what I should wear! Can you come up?"

She sprints up the steps, looking surprised that I want her opinion.

"Mom, you have to help me."

"Well, okay then. First put on your nice black slacks." She goes to my closet to get them and I put them on. "I'll find a blouse," she says, rummaging through my closet. She hands me my pearly-sheen white one and follows it with my velveteen jacket, saying, "Wear this over it."

When I'm ready, she looks me over: "All you need are some simple earrings and understated makeup. Be businesslike." I follow her advice, grateful that she can still think straight. Not me; I'm too nervous to make even the simplest decisions. Finally she hands me a pair of her gold hoops. I put them on and I'm done. I walk down the stairs and Mom comes with me.

"Wow," says Michael, who's standing at the bottom of the stairs.

"She's transformed, isn't she!" Mom says to him.

I put on my coat as I'm running out the door.

"Yeah, instant makeover!" He laughs.

"Yup. Into a goddess," I say with a smile.

"Yes, 'goddess' definitely works," says Mom.

I hear Miss Sinclair's car pull up. "She's here!"

"Good luck," Mom shouts from the doorway.

"Go for it, Cass," Michael shouts. "Knock 'em dead!"

Miss Sinclair zooms onto the highway. When we reach Chicago, she heads to Lincoln Park and she finds a space near Amelia's townhouse.

I get out and slam the car door. It's colder than usual tonight and I forgot my gloves again. I force myself to take one step, then another, till somehow I get to Amelia's steep front stairs. At the elaborately carved wooden door I wait behind Miss Sinclair. She rings the doorbell as icy winds blow.

Inside, Amelia leads us to the same room as last time. But tonight she's not serving tea. We each sit in the same places as last time, as if the seats are reserved.

Miss Sinclair thanks Amelia for seeing us.

Amelia and I smile at each other. It's a promising start, but I'm terrified about what's coming next.

"So. Here we are," says Miss Sinclair, as she claps her hands together. She smiles as if we're getting ready to play charades.

"First, I want to apologize to you and Cassandra for taking such a long time to get back to you," says Amelia.

"We understand, Amelia," says Miss Sinclair. "It's an important decision."

"I know it must've been hard for you to wait, dear," she says, looking at me. "But I found this to be a very difficult decision to make."

"We understand that the Bergonzi's irreplaceable. It's a very rare, very valuable violin," says Miss Sinclair.

"But it's about more than just money, Eva," she says with some annoyance.

"I know that," says Miss Sinclair.

"What you don't know is"—she leans forward—"I'm going to be very honest with you both."

"We understand. What is it you want to tell us, Amelia?" Miss Sinclair asks.

Amelia turns to me and suddenly, it's like we're the only ones in the room. "What I want you to know is that I was abused as a child, Cassandra."

I gasp.

"I don't know your whole story, Cassandra. But what's remarkable to me is that even though your father destroyed your violin, you're somehow still able to play—and with a great deal of courage and passion, I might add."

"Thank you, Amelia. That means a lot to me."

"Your bravery makes me want to entrust my violin to you."

I can't help it. I start to cry.

"I want you to protect it with the same kind of power you have when you play it."

"I will. I promise!"

Miss Sinclair hands me a tissue.

"And another thing," Amelia says.

"Yes?" I ask, dabbing at my eyes.

"I want you to use it with great joy."

"Oh, Amelia! I definitely will!"

Now she gets up and comes over to me. We hug through tears. Amelia is short like Winnie. She's frail yet strong, both at the same time.

"The truth is, I wanted to have another chance to sit with you again, before I finally made up my mind."

I smile.

"There's something . . . ," Amelia continues, "I don't know what it is—but there's just something about you, Cassandra. I knew right away when you walked in tonight that I wanted you to have my violin."

"Thank you so much, Amelia. This means everything to me."

❖

Later, when we're back out on the sidewalk, Miss Sinclair puts her arm around me. We walk side by side, our steps falling in rhythm.

"I want to thank you, Cassie."

"Me? What for?"

"For reminding me of something very important."

"What's that?"

"To always be honest, no matter what the consequence."

"Okay, Miss Sinclair. You're welcome."

I think back to the train station, when I felt so ugly telling Nick what Dad had done. Both times, telling the truth worked out better than I expected. And now I'm starting to feel really good.

We continue walking in silence to the car. In the sky, I see a crescent moon. Beside it is a diamondlike star; it's twinkling. I clutch my new violin closer, feeling its weight. It makes me feel whole again—a Violin Girl once more.

CODA

It's sort of like Nick never left. Well, what I'm trying to say is that it's like he fits here perfectly. He fits right into my life. His parents let him come to Chicago right after Christmas, almost a week earlier than we'd planned. He's here to help out with my benefit concert for the same homeless shelter where I spent that night when I ran away. The concert's tonight, on New Year's Eve.

Nick gets along well with Michael. And he knows how to handle Mom's intensity. I was a little worried about what would happen with him and Dad, since Nick was pretty mad at Dad for what he did to me. But that turned out okay, too. I told Nick what Dad revealed in our family therapy session—about what my grandfather did to him. Nick's cool with the fact that my dad seems to be trying, so he's keeping an open mind about him. And my friends are all crazy about Nick—which reminds me: I want to make sure he and Ariel are never alone at the party after the benefit. They'd make way too great of a couple.

At four, we all pile into Mom's car. I hang up my new outfit in the backseat area so it won't get crushed. Then I sit beside Nick and cling to my Bergonzi with all my might.

Mom pulls up alongside Unity Temple and Winnie's pastor meets us at the door. Inside, Dad's waiting for us with a bunch of Michael's buddies who've signed on to help out with the setup. Like a small army, they work moving amps and microphones, connecting wires and turning the sanctuary into a stage. When it's all ready, I stand to the side, looking out at the crowd. I'm hoping we fill every seat. It means more money for the homeless.

Winnie and I signed up so many musicians between us that we have enough performers for at least a two-hour concert. Miss Sinclair will act as emcee, announcing each of the acts. Winnie's mom and dad will take tickets, and their friends from the church will be ushers and hand out the programs. Winnie got her graphics class to make them for us and they look awesome.

I run around like I know what I'm doing, which I actually don't. Then Winnie starts to spaz out when she finds out some programs are blanks. But I grab her wrist and say, "Win, will you breathe, please? Okay?"

She glares at me like she wants to kill me. But I want to calm her down.

"Here's the thing, Win. It doesn't matter if everything's not perfect."

She furrows her brow. "It doesn't?"

"No! What's important is that we're trying to make a difference. You know—we're doing *something* to help the homeless. Just think about that instead of it all having to be perfect."

She exhales. "You're right." She throws out the blank programs and relaxes a bit.

We're busy right up until it's time to start the program. Then Miss Sinclair walks to the center of the stage and begins. "I want to welcome everyone to our benefit concert for Hannah's House, a homeless shelter for teenage girls."

The audience applauds.

"We're grateful to Unity Temple for hosting us tonight in their wonderful house of worship. We've got a marvelous program in store for you—a fine group of young musicians who are waiting to entertain you. And since you're not here to listen to me, let's get started."

I hear the applause and it makes my heart speed up. I check the mirror once more in our make-shift dressing room. I'm wearing my interpretation of a goddess outfit: a long flowing skirt and a silky top, its ruffles etched in gold. My hair's pulled back, showing off the crystal earrings Nick gave me for Christmas.

Winnie comes in and looks at me through the mirror. She says, "You really do *look* divine."

Smiling at her, my jitters go away.

When I hear my name announced, I glide out on stage in my ballet flats. The place is packed. Soft light warms the wooden pews. Mom and Dad are sitting in the front row. Getting into my starting pose, I see Dad grab Mom's hand. Michael winks at me. Behind them sits Amelia, beaming at me with great pleasure. When I told her about the benefit, she made a substantial donation and said she was proud of me for having this be the debut performance for me and the Bergonzi.

I know the program says I'll be performing Mendelssohn first, but instead I start off with "Here Comes the Sun," by the Beatles—it's Nick's favorite song. I picked a great arrangement and I love the way it winds and drifts, almost like a lullaby. Between the deep tones of the Bergonzi and the acoustics in this soaring space, the piece sounds almost otherworldly.

Settling into it, I peer out into the pews. A few rows behind Amelia, I find Nick in the third row, right in the very center. He looks surprised and happy, and he knows this song is for him. On and on, I play, talking to him through the notes. Goddess music calls to his baseball soul. I'm at my own version of home plate. Trusting my hands, I'm taking a swing.

Bow on string, like bat to ball.

I'm playing on.

Acknowledgments

The journey to this book was filled with wonderful people and I acknowledge and thank each one for being a light, a map, guiding me in remarkable ways:

Jenny Cappelli, violinist and teacher, was "on call" for many years and graciously answered any and all violin questions; Joseph Cali at Kagan and Gaines Music Company researched and suggested the Carlo Bergonzi violin for Cassie. Hannah Provenza educated me about the violin in the bleachers at a little league baseball game and gave feedback on a first draft. My sister, Joey Brenneman, and Deborah Roth clarified information on the Unitarian Universalist Church and on goddesses.

Karen Osborne made a safe space to study writing in her class and invited me to join her critique group with Julia Buckley, Martha Whitehead, Cynthia Todd Quam, Karen Halvorsen Schreck, Lenora Rand, and Kae Penner-Howell. All read many drafts, were patient and generous, and best of all, provided good snacks.

My writing teachers at Vermont College blessed me with much wisdom and especially these lessons: Kathi Appelt (poetry is chocolate), Sharon Darrow (directions to Cassie's heart), Louise Hawes ("freewrite" and be brave), and Tim Wynne-Jones (out of the comfort zone is *the* place to be). Members of my very first residency workshop offered the perfect blend of honesty and encouragement. My Salon Sisters: you gifted me with some of the luckiest moments of my entire life. Immense gratitude to Angela

261

Morrison for being a brilliant postgrad revision tour guide, co-counselor, and cheerleader to the very last chapter; and Lynn Hazen, for also giving amazing feedback and for encouraging the search for the violin goddess.

I'm so grateful for Evelyn Fazio, my publisher, who gave my work her careful and passionate attention; and who shares the love of baseball and cats with me.

The Society of Children's Book Writers and Illustrators—especially its Illinois chapter and Oak Park network—sustains me with inspiration, opportunities, and playfulness. They made it possible for me to receive a manuscript critique with Stephen Fraser. His kind words and good advice were a much-needed boost.

My mother, Carol Brenneman, my late father, Fleet Brenneman, and my sisters, Paula Brenneman Schmid, Lisa Brenneman Martignetti, Laura Brenneman, and Joey Brenneman, offered me a chance to come from a family of dreamers. My in-laws, nieces, and nephews have lovingly widened the circle.

My son, Dan Baron, checked the baseball details for authenticity. Every day he makes me laugh and is my reason for being.

David Baron, my husband, faithfully read every last word, every time, gave psychiatric consultations for my characters (and me), and makes it possible for me to live a writer's life every day.